TOUCH OF DEATH

TEMPTING THE FATES BOOK TWO

ALICE WILDE

Print Edition | Touch of Death by Alice Wilde
©2023 Alice Wilde

All rights reserved. This book or parts thereof may not be reproduced in any form, stored in any retrieval system, or transmitted in any form by any means–electronic, mechanical, photocopy, recording, or otherwise—without prior written permission from the publisher, except in case of including brief passages for use in a review.

This is a work of fiction. Names, places, characters, and incidents are either the product of the author's imagination or are used fictitiously, and any resemblance to any actual persons, living or dead, organizations, events, or locales is entirely coincidental.

For permissions contact:
alicewildeauthor@gmail.com

ISBN: 9798390043080

To the lies we tell in love.

CONTENT WARNING

Dear Reader,

Thank you for picking up Touch of Death book two in Tempting the Fates. Please be aware that this is a dark, plot-heavy fantasy romance with multiple love interests. Each book will end on a cliffhanger until the series is complete.

Please be aware that this series may not be suitable for all audiences, and it is certainly not for all ages. If you choose to continue, please be prepared to encounter some language, mental/physical abuse, murder, kidnapping, violent behaviors, the mention of non-con and attempted non-con (not by the love interests), death, violence, choking, voyeurism, mutilation, monsters, gods, revenge, redemption, heartbreak, and descriptions that may otherwise trigger you.

However, you will also find a great deal of wonderful and strange characters as well as angst, slow burn romance and eventual spice (this is not a fade to black series), and a cast of characters that is met and built slowly over the course of the story. This series is also multiple POV, so please be aware that some chapters may overlap slightly.

All this being said, there may be other triggers within the series that I have not listed. The journey will not be an easy one for our characters, but it'll be worth it in the end.

Or so one can hope.

Now, are you ready to continue ... *Tempting the Fates?*

Alice

1

DEATH

I move quickly through the dark halls of my palace, the heavy heels of my boots thundering in my ears as they echo against the obsidian.

My home is nothing but an empty abyss, broken beyond repair without Hazel's presence here to warm it. To breathe life into it.

I have to force myself not to pause as I pass each of the paintings she hung throughout the halls. There is no time to waste if I am to find her soul before it fully crosses over and is lost to me forever.

Still, returning to my bedchamber, I cannot help but hesitate as I clench my jaw at the sight of Hazel's body lying lifeless on my bed. Even in death, she is the most beautiful creature I have ever known.

"I will not forsake you, little one," I murmur, leaning down to tenderly brush a stray hair from her face.

Though the color has drained from her lips and cheeks, heat still lingers on her skin. It makes my heart ache and my skin burn, only further serving to remind me of the life that I have stolen from her ... that *I* am the one who brought this upon her.

Straightening, I swallow back the rising hatred I feel toward myself and force myself to look away.

To focus.

I have sworn to save her soul and that is exactly what I intend to do.

Throwing open my wardrobe, I run my eyes over the garments within. This quest will require more than most, and I must be prepared for whatever and *whoever* may rise up to meet me.

I do not presume to think the Underworld will simply surrender Hazel to me. In fact, I expect nothing less than to sacrifice a great deal for her return. I would be foolish to think otherwise.

However, that also means I must make sure I carry more to bargain with.

Walking to the back of my wardrobe, I kneel to unlock a gold-trimmed chest. Inside are some of my most valuable possessions, including a full set of shadowsilk and a bag of gold obols.

Removing the inky garments, I rise and undress to change into them. Only, as I do, Hazel's small book, wrapped in wax paper and tied off with a red ribbon, falls from my pocket, hitting the floor with a soft thud.

I flinch, staring down at it as I am reminded of my failure to return it to her. This realization only serves to harden my resolve.

I will not fail her again.

Picking up the book, I set it aside with the bag of coins before changing into the shadowsilk. I savor the chill of the silken fabric against my skin, thankful that they should help stave off some of the Underworld's heat.

Turning away from the chest, I select several sturdier items from where they hang, slipping them on over my inner layers.

My base complete, I pull on a pair of leather bracers, boots, a chest piece, and gloves. I finish off my outfit by adding a heavy set of black chains draped over my shoulders and chest, as well as a thick, hooded cloak.

Satisfied with my choices, I grab the pouch of obols as well as the small book and tuck them both into my pockets.

As I bend to close the chest, my eyes catch on an obsidian dagger sheathed in black leather, and I hesitate for only a second before adding it to my gear. The Underworld is an unforgiving place, and the gods only know what else I will face down there, or what I will have to do for Hazel.

Exiting the wardrobe, I walk over to a wall of hanging masks to look them over, my gaze catching on one in particular.

The bone mask I wore the first time Hazel stumbled upon me that fateful night in the forest.

Taking it down from its hook, I turn it over in my hand as I snort softly to myself. It seems only fitting that I wear the mask she met me in; perhaps it will help bring us together once again too.

With my preparations complete, I turn to leave the room, pausing briefly to look at Hazel's lifeless form once more. My heart twists painfully in my chest, and I am overcome with the urge to touch her one last time, but I do not allow myself to.

Placing the mask over my face, I pull the hood of my cloak up around it as I sweep from the room.

The halls echo around me once again as I make my way toward the Valley of Death, and Knax. As soon as I cross the mists, I let out a sharp whistle across the field, searching the horizon for signs of the white stallion.

It only takes a moment before I hear a whinny and then the thunder of hooves as he gallops over a ridge, making his way toward me. Knax's coat gleams in the early morning light, his mane and tail flowing behind him, and I cannot help but smile at the sight.

"Good boy," I say, patting him as he slows to a stop before me and shakes his mane out with a snort. "Come, let us go save the little one together."

Without a moment's hesitation, I swing myself up onto Knax's back as I take a firm grip of his mane. Settling into position, I press the heels of my boots into his sides, and together, we set off across the valley.

As we draw closer to the far horizon, I lean forward, urging Knax to move faster. Immediately, I feel the shift of his muscles beneath me as his canter turns into a gallop, the thrum of his hooves quickening beneath us.

A wall of mist suddenly rises up before us, and I brace myself against Knax as his body tenses beneath me before soaring into the air, forcing our way into the mists of Chaos.

Everything goes dark for a moment, and then we burst out of the mists and onto a barren wasteland.

Smiling to myself, I turn Knax in a circle, searching the horizon yet again for our next point of entry.

"Over there," I shout, nudging the stallion forward as, once again, we set off, my cloak billowing out behind me as we race toward the Underworld.

Toward Hazel.

2

HAZEL

I gasp, only to find there's no air to breathe. My chest tightens as my lungs remain empty, burning to be filled again.

Panic sets in as I try to open my eyes but find myself unable to do so. I can't see, can't breathe, as I'm swallowed whole by nothing and everything at once.

Darkness clings to me, wrapping its cold fingers around me only to tear me asunder before forcing the pieces of what's left of me back together, over and over again.

Pain and love, joy and heartache, hope and desperation, every emotion I've ever known, courses through my body in exhilarating intensity, only to be ripped mercilessly from it the next moment.

Until nothing but a void is left in their wake, and I find myself drifting quietly along an endless current.

My thoughts fade, and I no longer struggle to breathe as I let the darkness take over.

No longer struggle to remember ...

There is nothing left for me to hold onto as the icy current pulls me down, down, down into its darkest depths and away from all that I once knew.

All that I once loved.

Coughing, my eyes fly open as I roll over onto my side, one long, rasping breath trying to fill my lungs with the air I so desperately need. I choke, the air thick with the stench of decay, making it hard to fully catch my breath.

Slowly, I manage to sit up, clutching at my still-heaving chest as I turn to take in the strange twilight of the world around me.

I do not know this place.

A chill races down my spine at the thought, and I wrap my arms around myself as I blink in confusion.

Am I still alive?

I shake my head at the thought. No, that's impossible. I may not remember much, but I do know *that*.

This place isn't meant for the living.

I frown as I try to wrap my mind around the fact that I know I'm dead, yet, I still *feel* so alive. That I'm not just some lost spirit wandering aimlessly through time and space.

At least, I don't think I am.

Looking up, I find nothing but sky above me, though *sky* may not be the right word for what I see.

Strange colors swirl amidst an expanse of darkness that tries to choke them out, churning like an endless sea as they try to reach for me ... only to be swallowed up by the misty void before they can.

Watching it makes me feel ill, and I soon find myself forced to tear my eyes away.

Dropping my gaze, I look down over the edge of the cliffside I'm lying next to instead. Instantly, my stomach and mind settle, despite the great height of the mountain that I've somehow found myself precariously perched upon.

Expansive plains stretch out far into the distance, a long, twisting river leads away from the foot of the mountain, splitting the land in two. The entire realm, at least as far as I can see, looks like it's been coated in a wash of sepia, from the trees and rocks to the very color of my skin.

Skin.

I glance down at my body, almost surprised to find that I still seem to have one. Holding my hands up in front of me, I frown as I turn them over and tentatively rub my fingertips together.

I can feel, but the sensation is odd, like a whisper of something I once knew intimately but is now nearly forgotten. There's a bitterness to the feeling, though even that seems to be dulled.

These thoughts, these *emotions*, are little more than words that carry but a distant memory of what they once meant to me.

Something is missing, though I do not know what that something is. It's as if every aspect of my being is disjointed, struggling to get to me from some far-off place.

From *before*.

Yet, the more I try to remember what that was and how I got here, the more my head screams at me to stop.

To give up.

To move forward.

To let go.

These thoughts have me clutching my chest again as pain stabs my heart, radiating through my body in such a way that I'm forced to curl in on myself to wait it out. When it finally subsides, I take several steadying breaths in an attempt to regain my composure as I push myself back up.

One thing is becoming increasingly obvious to me, my mind and heart are at odds with one another. My head swims, ordering me to forget, while my heart begs me to hold on ... to remember.

So far, it would seem my mind is winning, but I refuse to give up so easily. Not when what my heart remembers still feels so important.

Looking out over the plains, my eyes follow the winding river into the distance. The dark waters glow softly as they cut a stark path through the monotony of the barren landscape, though in warning or invitation, I do not know.

The haze and gloom of the scene seep into my vision, further clouding my mind and thoughts. It's as if a growing somberness has settled over everything, from the furthest blades of grass on the horizon to the innermost parts of my soul.

Another gust of wind suddenly kicks up around the

mountaintop, whipping strands of hair around my face just as I hear the crunch of footsteps behind me.

"Why, hello there," comes a soft voice, and I look over my shoulder to find a strange man crouched beside the ledge, eyeing me curiously. "What are you doing up here?"

"I don't know," I answer, blinking up at him as his head tilts slightly to one side. "I just woke up here."

"Here, let me help you down from there," he says, offering his hand to me.

My mind blanks as I stare at it for a long moment before finally reaching out to accept it. Almost as soon as his fingers close over my hand, I'm pulled off the rocky ledge and onto my feet.

The stranger drops my hand with a sharp intake of air, and for a split second a rush of nausea overwhelms me. The world spins, and I'm forced to close my eyes as I struggle to remain upright, as if my soul and body are connected by nothing but a thread.

Though I suppose they shouldn't be connected at all.

Cautiously, I open my eyes to find the stranger staring down at his hand with a furrowed brow.

"How did you get here?" the man asks, his gaze shifting to me. "Who brought you here?"

"I-I don't remember," I answer.

He raises an eyebrow at this, stepping back to get a better look at me, and I take my chance to do the same to him.

The stranger is at least a foot taller than me, thick golden curls falling heavily around an angelic face to frame piercingly blue eyes and a full set of lips. His expression is open and friendly, a slight smile playing at the corners of his mouth, and yet, there's a dark intensity to the way he looks at me.

Almost as if he knows something that I don't.

He allows me another minute to stare at him, but my mind is too foggy to piece anything more useful together.

"Come, mortal," he says, his eyes narrowing slightly on me before darting around the mountaintop, "let us quickly be gone from this place."

I nod, my mind blanking again as I allow him to lead me away from the ledge.

Taking one last look over my shoulder, I can't help but think that there's something I'm missing, *something* I've forgotten ... But the harder I try, the more my mind reels, and I suddenly find myself slipping on the loose rocks beneath my feet.

"Careful, you must focus on the way ahead," the stranger says, catching me before I hit the ground and quickly righting me again. "These paths are treacherous, even for the most skilled of my own kind. You're the first mortal I've ever found this far up the mountain ..."

He trails off, as if he's almost said too much, and we walk on in silence for several minutes before his eyes shift back to me.

"Tell me, mortal, what is your name?"

"My name," I repeat, my mind spinning at his question. "I-I don't know. What is yours?"

The man stops, grabbing my arm to turn me toward him, and I can't help but notice that he's careful not to touch my skin this time.

"Hermes," he answers, leaning toward me, "what do you mean you do not know your name?"

"I don't remember," I say, blinking up at him.

"What *do* you remember?" Hermes asks, his brow furrowing as his eyes search my face.

Again, I try to search my mind but simply end up shaking my head at him.

"Nothing," I answer. "I know that I had a life before, but that is all. Why?"

Hermes watches me for a few seconds longer before releasing me.

"Come, we must not waste any more time here," he says without answering my question, an edge to his voice. Turning on his heel, he continues on down the steep path, motioning for me to follow.

I trail after him, trying my best to remain focused on the placement of my feet instead of the questions filling my mind.

Something definitely isn't right, and I can't help but feel like that *something* has to do with me and my life before. Even as I think this, my mind reels, and I am forced to push the thought aside as I re-focus on the task ahead.

Hermes leads us along the narrow, winding path, pausing from time to time to ask me another question or help me navigate a particularly treacherous part of the mountain. However, all of his questions are met with the same answer ...

I don't remember.

Each time the words slip past my lips, I feel more and more confused by them.

Who am I?

It's as if my mind and body are disconnected, refusing to cooperate with each other no matter how badly I want them to.

I'm still struggling with Hermes' questions and my own confusion by the time we finally reach the foot of the mountain. The river glows in the distance, and I find myself suddenly fixated on it, my weary feet carrying me forward as if drawn to it.

Our narrow path merges with a much wider one as we draw closer to the river, and I suddenly notice an imposing figure standing by the water's edge. The hooded being is disturbingly tall and draped in layers of heavy, worn rags that drown out whatever form might lie beneath them.

Though the figure's back is to us, I sense that I should be wary of who or whatever it is. Hermes stiffens at my side, only confirming my suspicion, as I glance up and watch his jaw harden in uneasy silence the nearer we draw to the cloaked form.

"Hermes," comes a rasping voice, the sound scratching its way down my spine as the creature slowly turns toward us … and I find nothing but a gaping hole where a face should be staring back at us.

3

HAZEL

"Charon," Hermes says in a nervous greeting.

"What is the meaning of this? I have already carried today's souls across the river, as you well know."

Hermes shifts uncomfortably beside me at this.

"I know, but," my guide pauses for a moment, as if choosing his words carefully, before continuing, "this one is different."

"Different," Charon sneers, "how so?"

"She is still warm."

"Is that so?" Charon muses, the empty hood tilting as I feel his attention shift to me. "And what of her body? Where is it?"

"I must admit that I do not know."

Charon's silence is nearly as unsettling as the way Hermes refuses to meet my gaze as I glance between them. Yet again, I can't help but feel like something isn't right, but no one is willing to explain what is happening.

"What do you mean by that?" Charon finally asks, his gaze seeming to turn toward Hermes.

"I mean, her body, I could not locate it in the mortal realm."

"Impossible," Charon snorts, his hood shaking in disbelief. "Did you truly look, Hermes? We both know you have a tendency to be flighty, *especially* around this time of the year."

"Yes, I did," Hermes snaps, his fists clenching at his sides, "but there's only so much I can do when the girl does not even know her own name."

Charon pulls back slightly at this.

"What did you say?"

"The girl, she says that she remembers nothing of her life before, let alone how she got here."

I feel Charon's attention shift back to me, the empty hood tilting slightly to one side as if he's considering me in a new light. The weight of his gaze is heavy, sending shivers racing down my spine and across my skin as it bores into me.

"This mortal, where did you say you found her?"

"I did not—"

"Tell me *where*," Charon snaps.

"At the top of the mountain."

"You fool," Charon hisses at Hermes before stepping closer to me, a gnarled hand suddenly appearing from the depths of his many layers as he raises it out toward me.

My eyes catch on his hand, taking in the sallow skin stretched far too taut over twisted bones. I'm so distracted by the fact that there appears to be more to him than just floating rags that it takes me a moment to process that he's speaking to me.

"Give me your coin, girl," he demands, his voice dragging over my skin as if challenging me to disobey.

"Coin?" I ask, my brow furrowing as I absentmindedly pat myself down in search of one to offer him before glancing up at Hermes in confusion.

"See?" Hermes says. "No body, no coin, no *memory*."

"Of course, I see that, you imbecile," Charon hisses, cutting Hermes off as his hood snaps toward him. "Have you forgotten our orders when it comes to ... *living* souls?"

"No, but ... wait *that* is what she is?"

"Do you know what you have done, boy? She should never have left the alter! Gods be damned, I should toss *you* into the river for this."

"What are we supposed to do with her now?" Hermes asks nervously.

The ferryman sighs deeply, shaking his hood in thought.

"What has been set in motion cannot be undone. The mortal must be dealt with, but without a coin, there is only one thing left to do unless we both want to lose our heads over this."

"Charon, you cannot mean—"

"Silence, boy. You know the rules," Charon orders. "Now, get in my boat, mortal."

I move forward, unable to stop my feet from obeying the creature's demand.

"Be careful not to touch the water," he warns with a dark chuckle, stepping aside to let me past, just as a decaying boat materializes on the water. "We would not want you to get dragged under by the souls of the lost and the damned now, would we?"

My stomach twists at the thought as I reach for the stern of the boat to help me up, only to find my hand caught by Charon's twisted fingers instead.

A shudder runs through me, and I instinctively try to pull back, but his boney grip tightens to keep me in place. I inhale sharply as he leans closer with a hum of pleasure.

I glance up at him, my eyes widening as I take in a set of sharp, pointed teeth protruding from a grinning mouth that has suddenly appeared in the otherwise empty abyss of his hood.

I struggle to wrench my hand free, but Charon's grip is like iron, unyielding and relentless.

"Let go of me," I gasp, an icy chill creeping its way up my arm as what little warmth I have seems to drain from me.

"Why, my dear, I am only trying to help," he says, his voice dripping with honeyed venom. "You do not want to fall into the river, do you? The souls within are hungry, always looking for new ones to drag down into the depths."

I grit my teeth, fear and disgust rising sickeningly within me. My soul tugs at me, warning me not to trust this monster, but I have no means of escape.

Nowhere to go but forward.

No choice but to accept his help.

"Fine," I say, my voice barely audible as I tear my eyes away from Charon's hood, once again focusing on the dark rolling waters of the river.

"Good girl," the ferryman sneers as I begrudgingly allow him to help me.

As soon as his grip loosens on me, I hurry to scramble away from him, my heart racing as I settle onto one of the wooden seats. The boat rocks beneath me as Charon takes his place at the helm and pushes off from the shore.

"Good luck," Hermes calls, but he's already gone by the time I glance back at him.

I peer over the edge of the boat, the water writhing and churning beneath us, and I can't help but wonder what horrors lie below the surface.

"Are you sure this is safe?" I ask, the question slipping from me before I can bite my tongue.

"Nothing is safe here," Charon chuckles darkly. "Especially not for a mere mortal such as yourself."

We fall into an uneasy silence, broken only by the sound of sloshing water and the occasional creek of the boat, as Charon guides us further into the river.

"Where are you taking me?" I ask, my voice nearly swallowed up by the heaviness of the air.

"Now, now, do not bore me with such useless questions. You know very well where I am taking you, or rather, where the river is guiding us, whether or not your soul is willing to admit it. Come, ask me the question that is *really* on your mind."

I shiver at the way his voice crawls over my skin, and I can't bring myself to look back at him out of fear that he might have actually drawn closer.

"These souls you speak of," I start, my eyes dipping back to the black waters, "why are they stuck here?"

Charon laughs, the sound ringing out across the

water and causing the hairs on the back of my neck to stand on end.

"Why not try asking them yourself?" he whispers, his hood suddenly appearing next to my ear.

I cry out as his boney hand clamps down on my shoulder, and he forces me to lean out over the side of the rickety boat.

"Take a good look, mortal. Tell me wha—"

Charon's words are suddenly cut short as swirling shadows rise to throw us both back into the bottom of the boat.

The whinny of a horse carries across the water as I sit up. Turning, I see a giant white stallion rearing up on the shoreline as a rider dressed in all black holds on to his mane. The horse snorts as his hooves slam down into the muddy riverbank as those same inky shadows slither back to swirl up around it.

The rider straightens, his dark eyes flickering briefly to mine from behind an ornate bone mask before narrowing on Charon. Something within his gaze cuts me to my core and has my heart skipping a beat in my chest ... and yet, every instinct within me warns me against him.

"Death," Charon says with a dry chuckle, "what brings you to my humble river?"

The rider's name is ... Death?

I can't help the way my eyes widen as I put everything together. The pale horse, the midnight rider of shadow and ice, is quite *literally* death incarnate.

"The girl," Death shouts, my heart once again skipping a beat in my chest as the deep iciness of his voice sends chills racing down my spine and across my skin. "Give her over to me. Her soul is *mine*."

My heart thuds to a stop in my chest as *fear* suddenly takes over.

What life did I live before in which Death must still come for me here?

4

DEATH

"No," Charon finally answers, drawing himself up, "her soul belongs to the Underworld now. She has already boarded the ferry, and I have only one course of action left to take to fulfill my duties."

"Charon, do not test me," I growl in warning.

"Test you? I would not dare," Charon sneers, "I am simply stating the facts. You have already played your part, Death. Now, you must let me play mine."

"You seem to be forgetting yourself, Ferryman."

"It is *you* who forgets himself. The river's debt must be paid," Charon says, grabbing Hazel by a handful of her hair and dragging her back to the boat's edge, "and seeing as she has no coin to do so—"

"I will make you deal," I shout as I dismount Knax, my boots hitting the ground with a heavy thud. Anger burns in me at the sight of him touching her, and I have to force myself to remember that smiting him would only further seal Hazel's fate out there on the Styx.

"A deal with Death," Charon muses. "What do you propose?"

"I will pay her passage," I answer, "as well as my own. Simply ferry us across together, thus satisfying your duties and the river's debt. Then, you can return us to this side and allow her to leave with me."

"And if I refuse?"

"I will see to it that it is the last decision you ever make."

Charon's grip momentarily tightens in Hazel's hair before he finally releases her back into the boat, and I make note of all the ways I intend to make him pay for hurting her ... once she is safely away from here, of course.

"Fine," he says with a snort, "I will accept your deal ... under one condition."

"Which is?"

"You pay double the fee."

Disgust washes over me at this. Of course, I should have expected as much from the greedy demon.

"Very well," I say, reaching into my pocket to pull out four heavy gold coins.

Charon's eyes light up at the sight of them, and he nearly falls over himself as he scrambles to guide the boat back to shore.

My fingers close around the gold coins, my shadows twisting up around me as he draws closer. The only thing keeping me from unleashing my fury on him is the small huddled form of Hazel curled up in the bottom of his ferry.

Knax paws the ground behind me, his dislike for Charon only outranked by my own.

"The coins?" Charon presses as the boat runs aground.

"We must shake on the deal first," I say, stepping closer. "I would hate to think you were trying to find a way to back out of your end of the bargain."

I hold out my empty hand to him. Charon eyes it warily for a long moment before moving to the bow of the boat, his boney hand darting out to take mine.

The handshake is over in a matter of seconds, and yet, he still shivers at the frost that I allow to bite its way into him. I would almost be amused at his fear, if I was not already so focused on the future torment that I have planned for him.

Dropping the gold coins into his hand, Charon shrinks back.

"Let us be gone from here before I come to regret this decision more than I already do," the ferryman mutters, sizing me up as he tucks the coins into the folds of his cloak.

I hold my tongue as I climb into the boat, settling onto the bench across from where Hazel still cowers.

"Here, little one," I say softly, leaning forward to offer my hand to her, "let me help you back onto your seat."

Her eyes widen on me, but all she does is pull her knees closer to her chest. Charon pushes us away from the shore, and Hazel flinches as the boat rocks beneath us, ducking to bury her face in her arms.

It takes every bit of self-restraint within me not to reach for her, not to pull her to my chest and never let go.

It is only out of fear that she now hates me that I refrain from acting on this.

Sitting back, I try not to show how much this thought pains me as I stare out over the dark waters of the Styx. I will not force her to be with me, if that is not her wish.

Darkness closes in around us until the only light that remains is that of the single lantern hung from the bow, and we can longer see the shore, let alone the way ahead. Gradually, I feel eyes on me and glance back to find Hazel watching me. Her knitted brow worries me, until her eyes lift to meet mine ... and I finally understand what I am tasting in the air.

It is not hatred that stares back at me, but fear.

Fear, because she has *forgotten* me.

There is no warmth or recognition in her gaze, and it nearly shatters me to realize this. To know that, now, I alone hold the memories of our time together.

That I alone remember *us*.

Her soul still sings to me as it always has, but I was a fool to think that I made enough of an impression upon it to withstand the ravaging of death upon it.

But that is exactly why I am here. I will find a way to save her, a way to help her remember and live once more.

Whether or not she chooses to do so with me.

Charon's grumbling grows louder, interrupting my thoughts, and I clear my throat in warning ... which he chooses to ignore. His grumbling only grows louder as he complains about being forced to do more than double the work just to charter me back and forth across *his* river.

Annoyance burns in me as the minutes slip past, until I am unable to put up with his moaning a second longer.

"Enough, Charon," I growl, "I will have your silence. See to it, and I will give you two more coins for your trouble once we reach the other side."

As expected, this does the trick. He immediately brightens, straightening as he continues to guide us along the river, and I know he believes he has played me for a fool. Despite the heavy hood, I can still make out the flash of his satisfied grin as he begins to whistle a low, somber tune.

Training my eyes forward, I harden my jaw, determined not to give Charon the satisfaction of engaging with him any further. The sooner we get across this river and away from him, the better.

This is not the first time I have crossed the Styx, but today it seems to stretch on forever in the darkness. The ancient wood groans beneath us as the churning water grows more violent as the souls within fling themselves against the boat with ever-increasing fervor.

At long last, the darkness gives way to the muted colors of the opposite shoreline and a lantern-lit dock. I stifle a sigh of relief, unwilling to give Charon the pleasure of hearing it.

Soon, the first leg of our journey will be complete. I am eager to be rid of the ferryman and to finally have a moment alone with Hazel. I need to assure her that she is safe and that I fully intend to right the wrongs that I have acted upon her.

If she will but allow me.

"Brace yourselves," Charon says far too late as the

boat bumps roughly into place beside the dock. He anchors the ferry using his pole as a wedge before stepping up onto the pier and turning to offer his gnarled hand out to Hazel.

"What are you playing at Charon?" I ask.

"The river's debt," he answers. "For the ferry ride to count, you must both step from the boat."

I clench my teeth as I watch Hazel take his hand. Anger burns within me at the sight, though out of jealousy over him touching her or simply hatred for the demon himself, I do not know.

Rising from my seat to join them on the dock, I level Charon with a look before realizing Hazel has stiffened, her breaths hitching in her throat.

Turning to follow her gaze, I suddenly realize why Charon was so quick to accept my deal. A massive beast has emerged from the shadows of a nearby cluster of ruins, his eyes trained on us as he stalks toward the end of the dock.

Cerberus.

I step protectively toward Hazel as the hellhound lets out a low growl, his lip curling up to reveal fangs nearly the size of my hand.

"What the hell is he doing here?" I hiss.

"New rules," Charon calls out, the way his voice carries drawing my attention back to him.

"Damn you Charon, we had a deal," I shout, realizing he has already returned to his boat and pushed away from the dock, soft ripples marking his retreat back across the river Styx.

"Curse me all you like, but I never agreed to any time

frames. Now, I suggest you focus on dealing with *him* before it is too late for your little mortal," Charon chuckles darkly before vanishing into the dark.

As much as I cannot wait to make him pay for what he is done, Charon is right about me needing to find a way to deal with Cerberus.

There will be no going back otherwise ...

Not if I want to return with Hazel's soul intact.

5

HAZEL

Fear digs its claws in deeper as I realize I've been left alone, stuck between Death and this new monster ... and I don't know which of them I should fear more.

My heart pounds in my chest as the massive wolf watches me from his great height, the burning embers of his eyes set off by the inky contrast of his fur. His fangs glisten in the dim light, puffs of smoke leaking from between them with each snarl.

Blinking, I suddenly realize what, or rather *who*, he is as flashes of old stories flicker through my mind.

Cerberus, the Guardian of the Gates, and the Keeper of Souls. He's the one responsible for making sure souls *stay* in the Underworld.

Unlike the stories I've read about him, he only appears to have one head, though that doesn't make him any less terrifying. I have no doubt that he could tear me to pieces within seconds if he wanted to, and yet, I find myself strangely drawn to him even as he lets out another low growl of warning.

Without realizing it, I move forward. The creature blinks in surprise as I take another step toward him, his head cocking slightly to one side as I reach out to touch him. The tilt of his head catches the light of the lantern, glinting off a single sapphire ring hanging from the wolf's notched ear.

Before my fingertips have a chance to brush against his fur, a large, gloved hand wraps around my wrist.

"Do *not* touch him," Death says, pulling me back and out of reach of the snarling creature as a chill races up my arm at the man's touch.

"Why?" I ask, yanking my arm away from him as my heart skips a beat in my chest.

Death flinches and takes a step back, and I feel a strange sense of guilt over my reaction to him touching me.

"Because," he says carefully, "no mortal soul has ever escaped the Underworld after touching him."

"Have any mortal souls *ever* escaped the Underworld?" I ask, my brow furrowing as my mind swims.

"No, not after death," Death answers after a long pause.

My eyes narrow on him as I try to make sense of my racing heart and thoughts.

"Do I know you?" I ask, unable to bite my tongue before the question slips from me.

"You did, once."

I feel like a fool having even given voice to the question. Of course, after all, death is the *only* reason I'm here.

"Why are you here?"

Before he can answer, Cerberus lets out another growl, momentarily drawing our attention back to the end of the dock. I watch as the massive creature steps toward us, the wood groaning beneath his weight.

"Damn it," Death mutters, eyeing Cerberus warily as he takes another step onto the creaking dock. "I promise to answer all your questions in time, but it is not safe for us to do so here."

Spinning around, I scan our surroundings before sprinting to the far end of the dock. Dropping down, I lean over the edge to peer down into the black water, my own reflection staring back at me.

"Perhaps we could swim or allow the current to carry us further downstream?"

"You cannot swim the Styx; it is ..."

His voice trails off as I blink and find myself staring down into the face of an unknown woman. Faintly, I hear the muffled voice of Death in the distance as I lean closer, my mind fixated on the woman in the water.

Her eyes are closed, her expression peaceful as deep red hair floats in a soft halo around her face. I can't help but feel drawn to her as I watch and wonder what life she could have lived to end up here.

Suddenly, her eyes snap open, revealing a pair of empty sockets as she jerks toward the surface of the water. I scream as her mouth widens and long spindly fingers swipe at me, narrowly missing as a strong hand grabs me and pulls me back to safety.

The spell broken, I lay on the dock, watching in horror as the creature scrambles to get to me. Death doesn't so much as flinch, his shadows swirling up around him as he steps over me to slam the heel of his boot into the woman's face. She lets out a furious shriek of pain as she collapses backward and once again disappears into the depths of the Styx.

"Are you alright?" Death asks, quickly kneeling to pull my trembling body into his arms as he searches my face.

"I-I think so," I answer, still in shock, surprised to find the chill of his body against my own comforting. "What was *that*?"

"*That* is what happens to those who leave nothing but hatred behind in their wake. She is one of the damned, forced to guide other souls to their final resting place while unable to move on herself."

"Will she ever be able to move on?"

"Perhaps, if she can take another soul's place. It is the river of the *lost* and the damned, and *that* is exactly why you cannot swim these waters."

Another low growl and the shuddering of the dock have us both glance up as Cerberus crouches, his muscles gathering as if he's about to pounce.

"What do we do now?"

"We follow his lead, little one," he says, rising and helping me to my feet. "I promise no harm will come to you as long as I am by your side."

I have no choice but to trust him.

My mouth dry, and with nowhere to go but forward, I slowly turn to face the growling monster that awaits us.

Following Death's lead, I watch in surprise as Cerberus' growls quiet, and he backs away to allow us off the dock. It's only as we move further away from the river,

Cerberus following close behind us, that I realize what is happening.

We're being herded along a well-worn path toward the mouth of an enormous, ornate gate. A shiver runs down my spine at the sight of it, and I can't help the way fear settles over me again.

"Why are you here?" I ask, pausing just outside the open gate, much to the annoyance of Cerberus who growls in warning.

Death glances back over his shoulder to shoot a silencing look at the giant hellhound before turning to me.

"I thought I made that clear," he answers, his eyes searching my face. "I am here for *you*."

"But why? I'm already dead," I press. "Have you not already gotten what you wanted from me?"

Death turns and closes the distance between us, his inky shadows billowing up around us in a frosty wave as he towers over me. Immediately, I drop my eyes to my feet, inwardly chiding myself for daring to speak to him in such a way.

What was I thinking? Who am I to question *Death* himself?

A moment of silence passes between us before a gentle hand lifts my chin upward.

"No," he says as our eyes meet. "I could spend a thousand lifetimes with you, and it would never be enough. I am here, because I cannot bear to live another day without *you*, Hazel."

Hazel.

I gasp, stumbling forward into Death, as the fog

breaks in my mind and memories flood in to replace it at the sound of my name on his lips. Memories of his palace, my studio, Knax, and ... of course, *him*.

"Sydian?" I whisper so that only he can hear before realizing I should probably not speak my name for him here.

Death stiffens for a moment before his arms wrap around me, anchoring me to him.

"Yes, little one, I am here."

My chest tightens as I struggle to catch my breath amidst the cascade of emotions that well up within me. My heart breaks, tears spilling from me as I am forced to come to terms with everything that's happened.

The deal ... Father.

I pull back, blinking up at Death as he watches me from behind his mask. My emotions war within me, but it's worry and wariness that beat their way to the forefront as I glance around.

"Our deal," I whisper, "did it work? Was my father's life spared?"

"Yes."

I frown as confusion seeps into my thoughts.

"Then how do you plan to bring me home?" I ask. "If I'm dead, then is this not my home now?"

Death lets out a small sigh at this.

"I do not yet know how," he admits, "but I promise that I will do everything in my power to save you from this fate. I will not rest until I have found a way to make you safe and happy once more."

I smile up at him just as his eyes lift to look behind me. The next thing I know, Death has pulled me behind him, putting himself in the way of Cerberus' snapping jaws.

"No!"

The scream tears its way out of my throat as Cerberus latches on to Death's arm. Death lets out a moan of pain so visceral that it has me stumbling back in shock, my stomach knotting in terror.

And then, just as quickly, it's all over.

Cerberus releases his arm and steps back like nothing happened. I frown in confusion until Death turns to look back at me, cradling his arm, and I see the fear in his eyes.

"No, Hazel," Death shouts, glancing from me to Cerberus as he leaps past him to lunge at me. Shadows explode around Death to rush toward me, and the next thing I know, I'm hit by an inky wave of darkness that thrusts me out of Cerberus' path.

I roll to the ground, just barely looking up in time, as Cerberus yelps out in pain. A heavy chain has wrapped around his neck, Death pulling on it from the other side to force Cerberus away from me.

The massive wolf howls in frustration, tearing at the chain as Death uses Cerberus' distraction to throw himself against the closing gates. By the time the beast has torn the chain from his neck, Death has already shoved his way through with the help of his shadows.

"Try that again," Death says to Cerberus, his chest heaving as the gates swing shut behind him, "and I will tear the eyes from your head so that you may never look upon another soul again, let alone your master's face."

"Death," I sigh in relief as he steps over to offer me his

hand and help me up onto my feet, "I almost thought I'd lost you."

"I cannot be parted that easily from you. Not unless you wish it," he says. "Now, tell me, are you hurt, little one?"

"No," I answer with a shake of my head before realizing he's still cradling his other arm. "Are you?"

"It will pass."

"I can look at it for you. I've had to tend to my brother's wounds before."

"Your brother?"

"Well, stepbrother's," I say, correcting myself. "Please, I might be able to help."

Death watches me for a second before offering his arm out to me.

I take it gently, turning it over as I search for any sign of tearing or blood, but there's neither. The leather armor bound around his arm doesn't even have so much as a puncture mark.

"See," Death says, "there is nothing for you to worry about. You are my only concern."

"Okay," I say, choosing not to mention the way I feel him flinch at my touch. "What are we to do now?"

"The gate will not open again until Hades comes to unlock it," Death says with a frustrated sigh, glancing over his shoulder. "We have no choice but to continue on down the path, for now. Unless you would prefer that I continue fighting Cerberus for however long it takes that to happen."

I have to bite back a laugh when I realize he's being serious.

"No, let us walk," I answer, my eyes flickering to the beast's long fangs as he snarls at us just inside the gate.

Death nods, collecting his chain from the ground and re-arranging it over his body, and we continue on down the path with Cerberus growling at our backs ... Though he's careful to keep his distance.

"Why doesn't Cerberus seem to be afraid of you like the others are?"

"Because he is one of the few creatures that I cannot kill. There are not many, but he is among them."

"What makes him special?"

"He is a guardian," Death says, glancing down at me before continuing, "Cerberus is a keeper of souls, a task not entirely unlike my own. As such, he works outside the bounds of fate."

"So, neither of you can die?"

"It is not quite that simple, but no, we cannot die without certain conditions being met. However, we can be maimed, and often that is threat enough to keep us in check ... for a time."

We walk on in silence for several minutes while I try to process everything that he's just told me. I still don't quite understand how everything works, let alone how Death might still be able to kill things that are already part of the Underworld, but I decide against questioning it for now.

If nothing else, his words carry the added weight of caution for me. Perhaps simply being among the dead here isn't quite as final as I thought it was.

At least, not yet.

"Where does this path lead?" I ask in a hushed voice,

suddenly realizing that there must be a reason why Cerberus is herding us along it.

"To the Judges."

"Who?"

"This particular path leads to the Judges, those who are meant to decide the ultimate destination of your soul. Minos, Rhadamanthus, and Aeacus."

I frown at the unfamiliar names as I try to remember any stories that I might have read about them.

"And these Judges, what will happen once they've judged me?"

"That will not happen," he says firmly. "I will figure out a plan long before I allow that to happen."

"But if it did? If you can't?"

Death's silence stretches on long enough for discomfort to settle on my shoulders as I wait for his reply.

Unease knots my stomach as I shoot a nervous glance up at him, the low growls of Cerberus growing ever louder in the quiet. I can't help but wonder how Death plans to escape the monster when he seems hell-bent on making sure we follow the path.

"If I am unable to get you away from Cerberus, then I am afraid our time together will be at an end," Death says, his voice solemn. "Should you come to stand before the three judges, they will be forced to make a ruling on your soul. Then you would step beyond my reach, little one."

He doesn't expand upon what exactly this ruling entails or why it would part us, but he doesn't need to. I can imagine what he's left unsaid for myself.

I take in a shaky breath as I look up at him again.

"Then we can't let that happen," I say, keeping my voice soft. "All we need to do is come up with a plan. I'm sure we can think of something, together."

I can literally feel his surprise at my words as his shadows waft up around us. Death stares down at me, silence filling the space between us for a long moment. I worry that he's going to turn down my help, but then he gives me a small nod.

"You are more than welcome to help," he says with a soft chuckle. "In fact, I would be happy for it."

Warmth blossoms in my chest as I realize how gracious his acceptance of my help is. After all, how could my plans possibly compare to a being such as him?

I lean in conspiratorially toward him, and he responds by ducking his head toward me as I excitedly begin whispering various ideas to him. Unfortunately, it doesn't take long for me to realize the task before us is far more complicated than I realized.

Death is gentle in his rejection, but I'm obviously out of my element, and it shows as he carefully explains the holes that riddle each of my proposals. Frustration begins to creep in as I realize we are slowly running out of what little time we may have.

"Do not give up, little one," he says when I let out an exasperated sigh. "We will find a way."

Suddenly, it dawns on me. It's so simple that I almost feel foolish even to suggest it.

"Cerberus," I breathe excitedly, "he's a dog, right?"

"I suppose, in a sense, yes."

"Good, then perhaps we're going about this entirely the wrong way."

"How so?"

"Instead of treating him like some monster hellbent on carrying out his duties, what if we were to treat him like the dog he is?"

"In what way?" Death asks, eyeing me curiously as a smile tugs at the corners of my mouth.

"I was thinking ... fetch," I say before quickly explaining when he doesn't seem familiar with the concept. "We toss something like a stick that way for him to chase after and then slip off into that forest over there."

"Fetch?" Death muses, his eyes growing distant in thought as he follows the point of my finger.

I wait with bated breath for him to answer, though I more than half-expect him to shoot down this idea, too. The longer he remains quiet, the sillier my suggestion seems as it bounces around unchecked in my head. I bite my nip anxiously, suddenly worried that he simply cannot find the words to kindly tell me how stupid I am.

I should never have given voice to such a dumb idea.

"It is so *simple*," Death murmurs, missing the way I cringe at the word. "I think it may just work."

"Really?" I ask, hope blossoming in my chest.

"Yes, but there is just one problem."

My heart sinks at this, of course, I should have known better.

"What is it?"

"There are no sticks within reach," he answers. "I highly doubt Cerberus would take kindly to us veering that far off track, and I am not about to risk your safety to try."

"Oh."

I glance around us, realizing that he's right, and the hope that had blossomed to life within me starts to wither.

"What else do your mortal dogs like?"

I blink up at him as my mind races for answers.

"Um, food," I say quickly. "Meat and bones ..."

"Hmm, very well," Death says, suddenly turning as a deafening whistle escapes him.

Cerberus freezes, his head cocking to one side in confusion.

"Death?" I question nervously, glancing between them.

"Trust me, little one," Death says, his gaze fixed on Cerberus as he slowly lifts his hand to his face. My breath hitches as he pulls back his hood and carefully removes his bone mask, turning it over in his hand once before deftly hurling it a fair distance away.

For one horrifying second, nothing happens, but then Cerberus lets out a strangely playful yelp as he turns to race off after it.

"Quickly, now," Death says, a wave of relief washing over me as he grabs my hand and drags me toward the towering tree line.

6

HAZEL

I can still feel the ground shaking as Cerberus bounds after Death's mask, excited whimpers replacing his snarls as we step into the dark forest.

"Do not let go of my hand," Death says, his voice low and commanding as he guides me through the densely packed trees. "We must move quickly, and it would be best for us not to get separated from one another in these woods."

"And what would happen if we were to get separated?"

I cringe inwardly at the question, my curiosity getting the better of me.

"Nothing. I simply do not wish to lose you among the trees, little one."

I get the feeling that there's more to this than he's letting on. That there's a far more sinister reason behind the way he keeps me tucked so close to his side, especially given that we'd move so much faster if there was more space between us.

But I am unwilling to give voice to these observations. Not when my heart races with the thrill of his touch, even with the thick black leather of his gloves a constant barrier between us.

This close, his body practically drains me of what little warmth I have left, and yet, I could not care less. The very nearness of him has me burning for him in ways I can hardly imagine without blushing.

Death's icy shadows coil around us, darting off in random directions at odd intervals as if searching out the way ahead. As the minutes turn into hours, our pace never slowing, my body begins to grow weary despite my best efforts to keep up.

"Where are we going?" I ask when I start to worry that I won't be able to continue on much longer.

Death pauses, our footsteps quieting for a moment, as he turns to look down at me. I inhale sharply, once again taken aback by the terrifying intensity of his beauty against the backdrop of the darkening forest. I'm almost surprised my heart still dares to beat at the sight of him.

"I am taking you to Aglaia, City of the Gods," he answers before continuing on through the trees. "We should reach it by morning and hopefully find help somewhere within."

My eyes widen at the prospect of entering a city specifically made for the gods themselves. Nerves twist my stomach into knots as I wonder what such a place will be like.

I try my best to keep pace with Death, but this time I'm unable to keep my questions at bay.

"Have you visited Aglaia before?"

"On occasion," he says with a nod, "but only when absolutely necessary."

"When was the last time you visited?"

He's quiet for a long moment before answering, "A century ago, perhaps longer."

"What are they like, the gods?"

Again, he falls quietly into thought, the crunch of our footsteps the only sound left to fill my ears as I wait. When the silence stretches on for another minute, I tentatively glance up at his face to realize his expression has grown dark and brooding ... which only makes me all the more curious to hear his answer.

"They think very highly of themselves," he finally says, the tone of his voice making it clear how greatly his distaste for the gods is. "Most of them have spent far too many years being worshipped by you mortals to have any sense of decency left in them. I would not bring you into their midst if I thought there was another way."

The disdain on his face is enough for me to bite my tongue ... for a while.

Eventually, though, I can't help the way questions seem to slip from me. Death is quiet, always taking the time to gather his thoughts before replying, but he does his best to patiently answer every question that I ask.

At long last, the night yields to dawn, and I feel hope brighten in my chest with it. The wild forest begins to thin around us until the trees suddenly give way to a view that makes my steps falter.

I gasp, my eyes widening as I take in the vibrancy of the world beyond. Unlike the rest of the muted Underworld, the City of the Gods and its surroundings are practically overflowing with color ... many of which I have no name for.

Beyond the city wall, towering buildings rise up among a waterfall of hanging gardens and vast sprawling palaces. Aside from Death's own palace, I've never seen such strange, yet stunning, architecture in all my life. My eyes move from building to building as I realize each is different, but no less exquisite, from the last.

I could spend a lifetime admiring the palaces and taking in the lush, wild gardens that spill out all around them and not grow bored.

"Hazel?"

Death squeezes my hand gently and I blink up at him to realize he's waiting for me. I blush, knowing my eyes are still wide with wonder, but he offers me a small smile in return. It's enough to melt my heart along with the apprehension that's started to settle into my bones.

"I'm sorry," I say, looking out over the city once again. "It's just so much to take in."

Despite what I've already seen here, somehow, this city is what makes the reality of my death truly hit home.

Death steps between me and the city so that I'm forced to look up into his face instead. He reaches up, cupping my cheek in the soft leather of his glove as his eyes meet mine. His expression is serious, the sharp angles of his face striking in their intensity as he searches for his words.

"The gods," he says carefully, "I do not know how they will react to you entering the city. This is their home, and never before has a mortal set foot in it. I cannot promise that they will listen to me, let alone provide help."

"I understand," I say.

"Hazel ..." He pauses, his jaw momentarily hardening. "Hazel, I need you to be prepared for the worst."

"The worst?"

My chest tightens as I stare up at him. I try to remain positive despite the flicker of sorrow that softens his eyes.

"It is entirely possible that they will make things ... difficult for us once I make my request."

I try not to let my imagination run wild at this as I nod in understanding. This could be it, the end of our time together. Should the gods be unwilling, then I don't know how it will be possible for us to have a future.

As much as I want to spend the rest of my life with him, whatever happens, I'll be forever thankful for the few moments we've been given. The very fact he chased my soul into death is more than I could have ever asked from anyone.

Death reminded me what it feels like to be loved, something I hadn't felt so deeply in the years since Merelda came into my life.

"If that turns out to be the case," Death says, drawing my attention back to him as he steps back to tear a piece of fabric from the bottom of his shirt, "I need you to know that I will do whatever it takes to protect you, and I cannot promise that there will be no bloodshed by the time I am through."

Death starts to lift the piece of fabric to his face as he turns back toward the city, but I reach out for him, stopping him in his tracks. He glances back at me, our eyes meeting as his head cocks to one side in question.

"Death," I start, my mouth running dry as I struggle

to give voice to my thoughts.

"What is it, little one?"

I open my mouth, but nothing comes out. Frozen here, between the forest and the city, I want nothing more than to profess my love for him ... to ask him to touch me, to press my lips to his once more, but I suddenly find I lack the courage.

I'm terrified that asking this of him will only result in rejection; only confirm that we *still* cannot be together.

Even if I would die a thousand times over just for one more kiss from Death.

One touch.

"Nothing," I say softly, giving him a soft smile. "I'm ready now."

I'm not sure if I'm relieved or disappointed when he watches me for a moment longer but doesn't push me to say more.

Tying the black strip of fabric around his face in a makeshift mask, Death pulls the hood of his cloak up, once again shrouding himself in darkness.

"Come," he says as he reaches to pull me to his side, tucking me against him as he covers me in his cloak, "let us conquer this city together."

I smile at this, the chill emanating from him a steadying reminder that he is *Death*. That despite everything we are up against, despite the fact that we are about to face the gods of the Underworld, I have to believe that his title, his position, is enough to give us a chance at forging a future together.

That this is not our last moment together, and I refuse to allow myself to think otherwise.

7

DEATH

It has taken every ounce of self-control I have left to my name not to pull her into my arms and kiss her. I am desperate to touch her, to feel the burn of her skin pressed against mine. To worship her completely, body and soul alike.

Desperate to tell her how deeply I have come to love her.

But all that will have to wait.

I cannot let on just how much she means to me here among these cretins that call themselves gods. The very fact I am here with her, for her, is already damning enough without letting on that I love her.

I must think of a reason for my being here. A reason for risking so much for a mortal soul that does not draw attention to my feelings for her.

Struggling to maintain my composure, I pull Hazel closer to my side, hiding her as best I can within the heavy folds of my cloak. I can feel the shiver of her body against mine and cannot help but worry. I hate that I am causing her discomfort, but I do not want to risk the city's inhabitants seeing her.

Not yet.

As we draw closer to the city, my eyes keep slipping to her. Hazel has only grown even more beautiful in death. Her skin glows softly, like crushed pearls beneath moonlight, the true loveliness of her soul put on display for all to see.

Her warmth and kindness make her burn ever-brighter in this world of darkness, chasing away my own shadows and leaving me in awe of her very presence. I can hardly believe she is once again by my side, and yet, it terrifies me that she is.

In this city of nightmares, her soul is a prize worth risking death for.

I should know.

If the gods see in her what I do, they will be reluctant to let her go from here without leaving them sated.

Especially if they realize *why* I want her soul returned.

They would ruin her, feed upon her soul until she was drained of all that was good and pure in her. Then, they would grow bored of her. She would be cast out to wander aimlessly, a shell of the woman she once was.

I clench my jaw at these thoughts, dismissing them from my mind. I will not allow that to happen.

I will find a way to save her, to save her from all of this and give her the life that she truly deserves. She will never want for love or affection again. For as long as the Fates allow, I will do whatever it takes to make her life wonderful.

The Fates.

I grimace at the thought of them. The gods will be the least of my worries if they find out I am here, let alone for what reason. The Fates are one of the few beings whom even I cannot kill; whereas I can manipulate life and death, they manipulate the course of humanity itself.

I am the only being in existence capable of destroying their plans with a single touch, and they have always hated me for it. If they found out my reason for being here, if they found out about Hazel, I do not doubt that they would try to use her against me.

Fortunately for me, I have always found fate to be a fickle thing, and I have already gone so far against nature that it will take time for the Fates to work out exactly what I have done.

And hopefully, that will not happen until Hazel and I are safely out of their reach.

With a small sigh, I harden my resolve.

No matter what it takes, I will save Hazel from her fate. I cannot depend on anyone but myself, not until I have exhausted every option to save her. But, for now, I must focus on winning over the gods. I have no fear of them; however, I must be careful.

For Hazel's sake.

The gods' palaces are dangerous, each one a reflection of the one who inhabits it. If I want to keep Hazel safe, I will have to remain vigilant.

Entering through the city gates, Hazel lets out a small sound of awe as she takes everything in. I smile at her wonder, but keep my eyes set on our destination.

Far in the distance, rising above the rest of the city, is

a towering palace made of sapphire so dark it is almost black. There, sitting within its glimmering halls, is the one man who holds the keys to this realm and to Hazel's freedom.

Hades, the God of the Underworld himself...

And an absolute prick.

8

HAZEL

As we move deeper and deeper into the city, I find myself pressing closer to Death.

Strange creatures, unlike anything I've ever read or even imagined, pass us as they go about their lives. My eyes widen as I take in the formidable beings with a healthy amount of reverent fear.

Most look almost human at first glance until I notice their horns, tails, or wings as they tower over me. Some are much smaller and more creature-like, while still others don't look human at all. They come in every shape, size, and color I could ever imagine, and I'm left staring in awe with each step we take.

So far, no one seems to have spotted me, and I don't know if that should worry me. The last thing I need is to be suddenly discovered and cause an uproar in the midst of all these creatures.

It's only now that I notice the way the city's inhabitants seem to give us a wide berth as they scurry past us. Glancing up, I realize that, to them, Death is the most frightening of them all. Even here, he stands out, towering above the rest as his inky shadows waft up around us as we walk.

I smile to myself at this. To think that I alone can walk with Death and not be afraid. Even if our story were to end here, in this city, I will never forget the way he's made me feel. The way my heart beats for him, and him alone.

Still, with each step forward, wariness begins to weigh on me, as if the city itself can tell that I do not belong here. As if it's watching, waiting for its chance to tear me apart.

I am still just a mortal among gods, after all.

Death's grip tightens on me as if sensing this, only intensifying my growing fear.

Swallowing past the lump in my throat, I steal a glance up at him, but his eyes remain trained forward. His silence does little to comfort me and instead bears down on me as I wait for him to say something reassuring.

But he stays quiet.

The ground beneath us begins to slope upward, and I suddenly feel more eyes on us as the gardens grow more expansive and the palaces even grander. I can't help but wonder if even the gods live among their own tiers.

Looking around, I realize there are far fewer beings roaming this part of the city, but those that I do see are even more breathtakingly intimidating than the ones before. These creatures carry weight to their presence in a way the others did not.

It suddenly dawns on me that, although this is the

City of the Gods, maybe not all the creatures that live here are *actually* gods.

Have we only just now entered the gods' quarters? Have we even reached them yet?

Death doesn't stop, his pace only quickening as more and more attention shifts toward us. The slope beneath our feet gives way to a wide set of stairs as we step through an archway, and then I see it.

A menacing palace that glitters with the sparkle of sapphire looms tall and imposing at the end of the long stairway. As we climb, I crane my neck to look up at the seemingly endless spires that reach far into the chaos of the sky.

Unlike the rest of the city, this palace isn't surrounded by beautiful gardens. Instead, twisted thorns and wilted flowers fill the grounds and courtyard leading up to the main doors.

As does an uneasy silence.

It isn't until we approach the wide-open doors of the main entrance that the silence is broken as a breeze carries strange whispers to my ears. Words that I can barely make out over the pounding of my heart. There's something off about this place, and I shudder to think what awaits us within.

Death guides me forward, but before we can step through the doors, two giant guards made entirely of stone suddenly step into our path. They tower over us both, gleaming obsidian swords strapped to their backs as they cross their arms over their chests.

As foreboding as they are, I almost let out a sigh of relief that we've been blocked from entering the palace.

"State your business," one of the stone guards says, his voice deep and reverberating.

"And name," the other adds in the same voice.

Death is quiet for a moment as he briefly glances down at me, my unease only growing as I note the way the guards are eyeing him. In this moment, I want nothing more than for us to turn and leave this place, to pretend we were never here.

Before I can voice this thought, Death straightens to his full height, squaring his shoulders as his inky shadows whip up around us.

"*I* am Death," he answers in a low growl that sends shivers down my spine.

Instantly, the guards tense, their own unease suddenly apparent as they share a nervous look. Death's grip tightens on me, only sign that he's as aware of their reaction to his name as I am.

"And your business?"

"I am here to see Hades, God of the Underworld. I have a personal matter to discuss with him."

I gasp, my stomach twisting anxiously at the thought of going before Hades, but I should have guessed. Of course, Death would want to go straight to the Underworld's ruler for help, but I can't imagine Hades being the sort to lend it.

Although I bite my tongue to keep myself from saying as much, my small gasp seems to have given me away.

"You brought a mortal with you?" one of the guards asks, his stony gaze dropping to me.

Again, Death's grip tightens on me as he takes a step forward and pushes me slightly behind him.

"Yes," Death answers, dipping his chin to look up at them in challenge. "My business with Hades concerns her, and you would do well to announce my presence to your master *at once*. And I suggest you leave the girl out of it if you value your existence."

The two guards blink at him before the first guard leans in to whisper to the other. The second guard nods as the first speaks, then, without a word to us, he turns on his heel and disappears into the palace behind him.

The first guard returns his cold gaze to us, silence wrapping around us as he glares down at me, and it takes everything in me not to flinch away from his stare. Until I realize the guard has shifted slightly to put more distance between himself and Death.

Of course, if he can't look Death in the eye, I'm the obvious second choice. Thankfully, it doesn't take long for the second guard to return.

"You have been granted an audience," he announces. "Hades awaits you in the throne room."

"Of course he does," Death says with a deep sigh.

Nodding once to the guard, Death takes my hand and pushes past the two stone warriors as they quickly step to either side. I flinch the moment my feet hit the crystal of the palace floors, but I keep my mouth shut as Death leads the way through the vast halls with a familiarity that suggests he's been here many times before.

Turning a corner, I find a cavernous room lying before us full of curious creatures in elaborate and strange dress.

"Get behind me, little one," Death whispers, and I

quickly do as he says, hiding myself within the drape of his cloak.

Quiet falls, the heavy thud of Death's boots echoing through the room, and drowning out my own softer tread, as we move deeper into their midst. One by one, those gathered in the hall turn to look our way before pulling back, the terror in their eyes as clear as day.

"Death," a low voice drawls, dragging my attention away from the crowd as they part to reveal a giant man lounging on a throne of jagged sapphire that almost looks too small for him. "You look so pretty in a half-mask that I almost mistook you for one of my own harem."

The man flashes Death a cold smile, his blue eyes narrowing on him from beneath dark brows. It's immediately clear to me that this man is Hades, despite the fact he looks nothing like how I imagined him.

Unlike the stories, Hades is disturbingly beautiful. His face otherworldly, callous and unyielding, in its allure. His features are strong and hard but nowhere near as striking as Death's marbled perfection.

Despite the chill of Hades' palace, he appears to be sweating from the way his shirt clings to his chest and shoulders, showcasing the strength that lies beneath.

"Hades," Death says in greeting, refusing to acknowledge the slight.

"Imagine my surprise," Hades continues, leaning forward in his chair so that the deep V of his shirt falls open to reveal the hardened muscles of his chest, "upon hearing that Death was at my doorstep, so far from home, requesting an audience with *me*."

Death's jaw hardens, but he remains quiet as he waits for Hades to finish.

So, what brings you to my humble little court?"

Clearing his throat, Death steps forward, and I can't help noticing how even Hades recoils slightly at this. The whole room seems to be holding its breath as it waits for Death's response. Slowly, I watch those gathered lean forward in growing anticipation.

"I have come to ask for a favor."

Hades sits back, clearly surprised by this.

"A favor?" he says after a moment, an eyebrow arching. "It would appear the Fates are smiling upon me once again. It is no small thing to have Death himself owe one a favor. This must be a terrible request indeed."

A smattering of nervous laughter ripples through the room at this, though I don't understand what he said that was so funny.

Death doesn't move, though I can feel his rage building in the way his shadows whirl up around my ankles. I shift slightly, letting out an involuntarily squeal as an icy tendril swirls up beneath my skirt.

Hades is on his feet in an instant, his form suddenly far more intimidating as his dark hair bursts into blue flames that lick their way down his neck and shoulders.

"What is the meaning of this?" Hades roars. "What have you brought into my court in secret? Answer me!"

"A mortal," Death says after a long pause.

"What? Show it to me."

Hesitantly, Death steps aside, unveiling me from his cloak.

Hades' eyes shift to take me in, raking over every inch

of my form in a way I am all too familiar with from men like him. It takes everything in me not to wrap my arms around myself in an attempt to hide from his stare as his face twists, his lips curling up in a wicked grin.

"Tell me, Death, what is this favor you ask of me?" Hades asks, the flames dying down to smolder around the edges of his being.

My stomach twists at the tone of his voice. It's the same one Amadeus and Merelda used on me whenever they were trying to bait me.

I don't need to hear the rest of the conversation to know where this is going. Hades has already made up his mind about me, and nothing Death or I can say will change that.

"Release Hazel Godwin's soul to me so that I can fulfill a promise."

Silence echoes through the hall following Death's words. Then, Hades lets out a rumbling laugh that seems to bounce off every jagged corner of the room. It doesn't take long for the rest of his court to join in with his laughter.

Still, Death stands tall, unwavering in his stoicism as he awaits an answer from Hades.

"A promise involving a girl's soul? My, my, you *must* have been lonely," Hades finally says with a sneer before gesturing toward the court. "No, I will not allow it. She is but a mortal. What would the others think if I were to grant such a ridiculous request? That they, too, can cheat Death himself with but a bit of seduction? Tell me, was she a good enough lay—"

"We have not lain together," I snap, rage burning

through my veins like a searing inferno. Before I can think twice, I take a step forward, my hands clenching at my sides as I draw myself up to my full height.

Hades cocks his head to one side, seemingly unfazed by my wrath, as an amused expression plays on his face. Still, I don't let that stop me as I narrow my eyes on him, my heart pounding in my chest.

"I spent my entire life trying to do what was right by others," I continue, "and I will not have my name slandered in such a way, *especially* not by the likes of you."

Hades draws back for a second before moving to close the distance between us. He reaches for my chin but pulls back before he can touch me as Death quickly steps into place by my side. I feel sick as their energies mix, crashing over me in a wash of ice and hate.

My body trembles, but I force myself to stand tall even as Hades towers before me. I will not allow him to intimidate me, not when I have Death on my side.

"Fascinating," Hades says with a wry smile, "tell me then, mortal, how is it exactly that you earned Death's favor then without giving yourself to him? Let me decide if your soul is somehow *worthy* of saving."

Swallowing past the lump in my throat, I glance nervously up at Death. He nods once, his face still neutral, and I take a steadying breath.

It still takes me a moment to find the words I need, my chest tight as I am reminded of the life I left behind. Of my father and what I gave up to save him with as few details as possible to still convey my story, careful to leave out my feelings for Death, and what I can only hope he feels for me.

Hades listens, his head cocked to one side, his expression unreadable.

When I fall quiet again, the silence is nearly deafening as he considers what I've just told him.

"Hmm," he says with a nod before turning to return to his throne.

I can't help the small sigh of relief that escapes me as I watch him settle into it. His eyes rake over Death and me before gliding over the rest of his court, and I can feel their silent anticipation as we all wait for his final decision.

My chest tightens, hope intertwining with a sense of overwhelming dread that he will still not help us.

I hate that so much is riding on him, or any of these arrogant gods that Death seems to despise so much. And yet, all I can do is wait and pray that they will find it in their hearts to show mercy.

After what feels like an eternity, Hades' gaze returns to Death.

"Guilt must weigh terribly on you, Death, for you to stoop so low for a mere mortal soul. However, as fascinating as whatever *this* is, I see no compelling reason to give her back. She would only have to eventually return anyway," he says with a sneer and wave of his hand. "Your deal was carried out as agreed upon, and now she is one of mine. The girl stays, so I suggest you enjoy what little time you have left together. As soon as I find out where that damned dog is, the mortal's time here finished … At least, with you."

Disappointment stabs me like a dagger to my gut.

"Come," Death says with an impatient snort as he wastes no time reaching for me.

"Enjoy your time in the city," Hades calls out with a dark chuckle as I'm all but dragged out of the throne room.

9

HADES

So, Death has returned.
I was almost beginning to think that he would not show his face again until it was too late. I snort to myself as I realize how easy he has made things for me without even realizing it.

Raising one hand, I motion for one of my guards.

"Yes, my king?"

"Inform your men that Death will be visiting our city for the indefinite future."

"Of course, my king," the stone knight says with a nod of his head. "At once."

"Wait, and send for Eris, as well. I will meet her at our usual place."

"And if she will not come?"

"Make her."

"Yes, my king."

The guard signals for another, and I watch as they exit the throne room before motioning for court to proceed.

One of my subjects steps up, blathering on about one thing or another, though all I really care about is the young woman huddled just behind him. I am about to say as much when something moves out of the corner of my eye, and I glance up to watch my wife slip from the room.

Frowning, I cock my head to the side as I watch her disappear from sight. A humorless smile tugs at the corner of my mouth as I suddenly rise, causing the entire room to kneel before me.

"I have heard enough; I have far more pressing matters to attend to. Court will reconvene tomorrow morning," I announce as I turn to leave before stopping to look down at the man kneeling at the bottom of the dais. "You, who is the girl with you?"

"My daughter."

"Then you must celebrate, for she is now one of my harem. Guard, have her prepped and brought to my chambers this night."

"Sire?" the subject asks just as one guard grabs the young woman. "She is already betrothed—"

I whirl on him, fire bursting along my spine as I slowly step toward him. His eyes fill with terror, and my smile widens.

"Did I ask? She is mine now; it would be best that you forget her. Return tomorrow, and you will be paid accordingly."

He remains silent as I stare down at him, and finally satisfied that he has learned his lesson, I move to leave again.

"My king, I would give anything, but please ... she is all I have."

I scoff, my lip curling up over my teeth as I turn and close the distance between us. Grabbing him by the neck, I lift the man up off the floor so that he can say nothing, do nothing, but claw at my hand.

"Now, you can say you gave everything for her, but to what end?" I hiss, clenching my hand around his throat so that his gasps become silent and his body falls limp. Dropping him, I wave disinterestedly at the man before ordering, "Put the body in the dungeon."

Leaving the throne room as the man is dragged out to the screams of his daughter, I make my way through the palace to one of the spire balconies that overlook the entire city.

It is not long before I hear the sound of struggle echoing up the stairs toward me. I watch the door as a guard appears and tosses a woman to the floor at my feet.

"Eris," I say, leaning back against the balustrade.

"Hades," she sneers, slowly lifting her eyes to meet mine. "To what do I owe the displeasure of being summoned?"

"Death."

She frowns, quickly scrambling back as she pushes herself up onto her knees. "What?"

"He has returned, and now we must make sure he stays long enough for everything to be put in place."

Her eyes widen at this, a wicked grin slowly spreading across her face.

"What do you require of me, my king," she says, her eyes bright with hunger.

"You are to follow him, find out where he goes and what he intends to do ... and this mortal of his, I would know how much she means to him."

"It would be my pleasure."

"You are not to harm the mortal, is that understood? She could prove to be useful."

Eris lets out a grumble of disappointment at this before answering, "Fine."

"Good," I say, turning to look out over my realm. "Now, leave me."

10

HAZEL

The silence between us is deafening as Death's boots echo off the crystal floor.

"Sydian," I whisper, careful that no one is near enough to hear, "what are we going to do now?"

The question, or perhaps the sound of my name for him, is enough to give him pause.

Though the throne room now lies somewhere behind us, we're still not free of the awful presence that fills this place. Death lets out a sigh as my eyes dart about the shifting shadows that seem to lean closer to us, as though they, too, are eager to hear what he has to say.

But Death says nothing.

The longer the silence stretches between us, the more I worry that this is it ... That *this* will be the end of us.

An end to something that's barely had a chance to start. I haven't even had the courage to tell him that my heart sings for him.

We have barely even had the chance to get started.

I've yet to even tell him the way my heart beats for him or how my fingers itch to capture his likeness again.

I open my mouth, but none of these thoughts slip out.

Nothing does, as Death suddenly pulls me toward the shadows, and I barely have time to react before he's wedged us both into a small crevice just off the main hall. His body presses against mine, making my heart beat wildly in my chest, even as his icy shadows rise up to shroud us where we hide.

Death lifts a finger to his lips, signaling for my silence, before turning to watch the hall. I follow his gaze, hardly daring to breathe given what little space there is between us, waiting to see what's caused us to suddenly take cover.

It takes a few more seconds before I hear the thud of approaching footsteps, and then I watch as several massive stone guards pass us by.

As soon as they're out of earshot, Death leans down so that his lips are as close to my ear as they can get.

I will not let Hades, or anyone else, stand in our way," he says, the deepness of his voice rumbling through me. "We still have time, Hazel. I promise that we will find a way yet."

Hope immediately bursts to life within me at this, especially when he pulls back just enough that we can look into each other's faces. Our eyes meet briefly before his gaze dips to my lips, and for one glorious second, I think he might actually kiss me.

My heart races, and I want nothing more than his touch in this moment. For him to give me some reassurance that he feels the same way I do about him. That him being here is because he loves me, and not simply out of guilt.

Death presses both palms into the wall on either side of me, his eyes searching my face.

"Hazel—"

Before he can say anything more, let alone kiss me, the soft clearing of a throat interrupts us. Immediately, I press myself back as flat as I can away from Death, my cheeks burning at the thought of being caught in such a state.

Nervously glancing toward the main hall, I find a small woman peering in at us curiously. She's breathtakingly beautiful, with delicate features and large green eyes that soften as they meet mine. Amusement pulls her lush lips into a smile as she takes a step toward us.

Death lets out a hiss of annoyance as he shifts away from me, his eyes narrowing on the woman.

"What are you doing here?" he demands, his voice coming out icier than I've ever heard.

The woman doesn't seem fazed by his tone as she lets out a small chuckle.

"I could ask you the same thing," she says, her voice somehow even more beautiful than her face. "After all, this is *my* home you are in."

Death tenses as she takes another step toward us.

"*Your* home?" I glance from her to Death and back in confusion.

"Yes," she says with a small nod, "I am Persephone, wife of Hades, whom I believe you have already had the absolute pleasure of being acquainted with."

"What do you want, Persephone?" Death asks, clearly irritated by her presence.

"I think I may just have a way to help you."

"Really?" I ask, hardly daring to believe her, especially when I can feel the skepticism rolling off Death in heavy waves. I don't even need to look at him to know he doesn't trust this woman as his shadows curl at our feet.

Still, I find myself curious to at least hear her out, and I find myself shifting forward without thinking. Death says nothing as the silence following her words stretches.

Finally, Persephone continues, "It won't be easy. In fact, it may very well be impossible ... This task that I believe will help you."

"Out with it," Death says, impatience making his voice gruff.

"Please," I add quickly, not wanting to scare off any help we might get.

Persephone smiles, "Find a way to convince *Cerberus* to let Hazel through."

"Impossible," Death immediately scoffs. "Cerberus is Hades' lapdog; you know that as well as anyone. There is no way—"

"Will you let me finish?" she asks, cutting him off with a single look.

Death falls silent, and I step closer, reaching for him in an attempt to calm him. His tension eases slightly at my touch, though his shadows continue to swirl in frustration around us.

I understand his frustration, given how our last encounter with Cerberus went. I don't see how this woman thinks we could possibly befriend him, but that only makes me all the more curious to find out what she has to say.

"Cerberus may be my husband's dog, but that does not mean that he cannot be swayed. Hades has grown cold as of late. He has forgotten who his friends are and where true power lies."

"What does that have to do with us?" Death demands.

"Hades needs to be put back in his place. Reminded of the god he once was," Persephone says carefully. "If you can find a way to win Cerberus to your side, to convince him that Hazel is worth his temporary disloyalty to my husband … it may just help shatter Hades' illusions of grandeur. If he can only be reminded that those around him require a leader and not a tyrant, then it very well might help the whole of the Underworld in more ways than one."

The goddess' eyes flicker to me as she says this, but Death doesn't seem convinced by what she's said. I cannot blame him either. What she asks of him, of us, involves a great deal of risk.

If she truly means to try to set us on a course to change the Underworld, I'm almost tempted to side with Death in his wariness. Even if denying her help would mean giving up the small flower of hope that's blossomed in my chest since her arrival.

"And how do you suggest we go about doing that?" Death asks.

"Well, it will not be easy, and it will take precious time," Persephone says.

"*Time* is one thing we do not have," Death hisses.

"Perhaps not, but at least I have given you a chance to save you *and* the girl before it is too late for her to return. Can you say you have a better plan?"

Death sighs deeply at this, his jaw hardening in thought.

"No," he says after a moment. "At least, not one that would not end in slaughter and damnation."

"Good, then we have until her body begins to decay to make this work," she says. "Otherwise, you know as well as I do that no task, no favor will be powerful enough to return her."

"I *know*," Death says, his shoulders tense as he glares down at Persephone. She doesn't so much as flinch at the chill wafting from him.

"Right, now, is the mortal's body somewhere ... safe?"

"Yes."

"And it remains unharmed?"

"Yes."

"Wait," I say, turning toward Death, "what is she talking about? How much time do we have?"

He says nothing, his eyes trained forward. I glance at Persephone, but all she does is shrug. Frowning, I turn back to search Death's face.

I realize he's been careful to avoid telling me that our time here has always been limited, though I suspect that was more for my sake than his. He never told me what he did with my body after my soul left it, either, though I haven't had the guts to ask him about it either.

"Death," I say, my voice soft, "where is my body?"

"On my bed," he says, finally glancing down at me.

"Oh."

I see the pain in his eyes as I reach for him, wrapping my arms around his body.

"I know it is morbid and that I should return it to your family, but I could not bring myself to part with it just yet. Not when the state of my realm gives us the best chance of saving you. Unlike the mortal realm, decay is not quite so ... predictable."

"How long does that give us?"

"It is hard to say, given the different workings of time and space among the realms. At the very least, ten days from death, though it is possible that your body will not decay at all as long as it remains in between."

Ten days.

Frustration hits me as I wonder how many days we might already have lost. Of course, nothing can just be simple. I take a second to get a handle on my emotions before forcing a small smile to my lips.

We are still together. There is still hope yet.

"Ten days is better than nothing," I say, brightening. "We'll just have to try our best to get back as quickly as possible."

Death stares at me for a moment before giving me a nod. Slowly, he forces himself to relax, and my smile becomes more genuine.

"Then we best not waste any more time," he says.

He moves toward the main hall, but Persephone continues to block his path where she stands at the entrance of the crevice.

"Step out of the way, Persephone," he says low in warning.

"Wait," she says, as Death makes an impatient sound, "I know someone who might be able to help you win Cerberus to your side."

"I do not need any help *winning* Cerberus over. I will make him see—"

"You will get nowhere with Cerberus using force," Persephone snaps. "You need to find a way to persuade him that letting the mortal's soul go is a noble act. Prove to him that his loyalty to Hades, his duty, is worth sacrificing for you."

"We do not have time for gentle persuasion. Cerberus—"

"I will *give* you time," she interrupts.

"How," Death hisses.

"Let me deal with my husband. I will find a way to keep Cerberus away from the city for as long as I can. In the meantime, I will take you to meet someone who will understand the weight of your bond and be willing to take a risk trying to save it."

"Who?"

"Anteros."

Death is still for a long moment as he considers her suggestion. I search my mind, but I can't seem to recall any stories about whoever they might be.

Biting back my curiosity, I wait patiently for Death to respond. Finally, he lets out a sigh.

"Very well, take us to him," he says with a wave of his hand.

Persephone smiles before turning to glance around the hall.

"Good. I will meet you in the city. Go to the bottom of the stairs and take the second alley on the left. Do not stop moving until I find you."

With that, she hurries out of sight.

11

HAZEL

As we slip out of the palace and make our way down the stairs leading back into the main part of the city, I continue to rack my mind for any knowledge I might have of Anteros. I'm starting to grow frustrated with myself for not paying more attention to the gods and their stories, but aside from my prayers and the occasional book that I helped father with, they rarely concerned me.

Especially when I had more pressing matters to consider, such as Merelda and her son.

Suddenly, it clicks.

Anteros, I know what he is the god of ... Love. True, requited love.

I frown, but how will he be able to help *us*? What did Persephone mean by saying that he would understand the weight of our bond?

Surely, she can't think that Death loves me.

Cares for me? Yes.

Feels guilty that my life was cut short? Sure.

But love? *True love?*

I shake my head. I would have to be a fool to think that.

How could someone like him possibly fall in love so fast, let alone ever consider someone like me his true love? After all, as everyone likes to keep pointing out, I am but a mortal, and he is ... *Death.*

He deserves someone who can spend an eternity by his side. Someone who won't be a hindrance to his power.

Someone he can actually touch.

She must not have meant it in the way I'm thinking, or perhaps I'm remembering things wrong. Perhaps Anteros is a different god entirely.

Perhaps he's not a god at all.

"Are you alright, little one?" Death asks, startling me out of my thoughts as we reach the bottom of the stairs.

"Yes," I answer quickly, giving him a small smile.

"Hmm."

He doesn't sound entirely convinced, but thankfully he doesn't press me on the matter as we turn down the small alley Persephone mentioned. The walls of two palaces line either side, flowering vines cascading over the tops to create a sort of canopy above us.

I'm still admiring their beauty when the small goddess steps out from a small niche to greet us. Her emerald eyes sparkle; the soft flush of her cheeks somehow made even prettier here amidst the blossoms.

"Quickly, follow me," she says, taking the lead as she begins detailing how she plans to convince Anteros to help us.

"I thought you said he would be *willing* to help," Death says coldly.

"Yes, but it never hurts to give someone more than one reason to help," she laughs. "The Fates must truly be smiling upon you because he owes me a favor."

"A favor for what?"

"For helping him realize his true love was right in front of his eyes. Thanks to me, he has never been happier or more in love than he is now."

Death makes a sound that only encourages her to continue as I try to think of something, anything to say to her.

Unaware of our silence, she continues, "Yes, it seems that even the God of Love can be blind to it at times. Funny, is it not, how we often do not notice what is staring us right in the face?"

So, I was right about who Anteros is.

I don't know what to make of the look she sends our way, but I have a hard time believing this simple favor will be enough to convince him to help us.

Silence once more wraps around us as we turn down several alleyways before stopping outside a set of extravagant golden gates.

Stopping outside the gates, Persephone turns to face us, her eyes flashing to Death's face before landing on me. She gives me a smile that I think is meant to be reassuring but only makes my heart pound harder.

I find myself unintentionally leaning forward, eager to hear whatever she's about to say. Hoping against hope that she might finally explain what she meant by her earlier comment.

"You must remember that in this city, each god rules over their own home," she pauses for a second to glance up at Death. "It would be best if the mortal were not to speak unless absolutely necessary."

"You need not worry about Hazel," Death answers, bristling at her words. "I can protect her."

"Things have changed since you were last here, Death. I would tread more carefully if I were you."

"I'll try my best to remain quiet," I say, breaking the tension between my two companions as they continue to stare each other down.

"Thank you," Persephone says with a gracious nod before turning to push open the gates.

She leads us through the main courtyard toward a pearly palace trimmed in gold with architecture so ornate it's almost too stunning to be real. I can't help the way my fingers itch to paint it.

The main doors stand wide open as Persephone steps through them without hindrance. There are no guards here, and my eyes widen to take in the way the sunlight filters through the glass ceiling to dance at our feet.

As we move further into the palace, I notice paintings hung along the walls. In my excitement, it takes me a moment to realize they're paintings of lovers in varying stages of undress and intimacy.

My cheeks burn as I quickly look away, focusing my eyes on the delicate pieces of furniture that fill the palace. I don't know why I'm shocked to see such depictions, especially in the God of Love's palace.

But, as we make our way deeper and deeper into the palace, I can't help but feel like something is off. I can't quite put my finger on it, though, as I glance nervously about.

Then, strange sounds make their way to my ears. Soft moans fill the air and drift lazily to us. Again, my cheeks flush as their intensity grows.

Just ahead of us, Persephone seems to hesitate, her cheery bounce all but disappearing as she comes to a large set of double doors.

She pushes them open before I can question whether or not we should, and I hesitantly follow her and Death inside.

My steps falter as I take in the scene before us. As soon as I realize what we've walked in on, I quickly train my eyes on the floor once more. It's still not enough of an escape as the sounds fill my ears to match the writhing of bodies at the edges of my vision.

My entire body burns with heat, and I wonder if it's too late to turn and flee away from the room. And yet, I can't help but peek at the scene unfolding around us as Death leads me further into the room.

There are strange and wonderful creatures everywhere I look. There are beings floating lazily in the air, others that slither or crawl about, and even some that look almost human.

Nearly all of them are fully engaged in intense lovemaking, some with more than one partner, while still others simply watch on from a distance as they work to satisfy themselves.

The way their bodies almost seem to move in rhythm with one another makes it look as if they're participating in some erotic dance. It doesn't seem to matter where I look; there's no escaping what I see.

I chew my bottom lip as the flame within me only seems to burn hotter and hotter with each passing second. Death pulls me closer, shifting to stand before me as if to protect me from the sight, the chill of his shadows helping to calm the fire within me.

"Anteros," Persephone calls out uncertainly, her voice barely rising above the noise of the room.

"Anteros?" comes a silken voice that's quickly followed by a soft laugh unlike anything I've ever heard before.

This laugh, this voice is intoxicating and somehow manages to ignite a new hunger within me. I feel drawn to it, unable to stop myself from wanting more.

Without realizing it, I find myself stepping out from behind Death, suddenly needing nothing more than to hear the voice again.

Death must understand what's happening before I do. He holds out a hand to stop me, his touch grounding me and allowing me to momentarily regain control of myself.

Still, I can't help peeking out around him as I look for the source of the voice.

In the center of the room, I find a throne of golden feathers beneath a domed canopy through which soft light filters, and sitting upon it, is one of the most striking beings I have ever lain eyes on. And I find it almost impossible *not* to stare at him.

The man's hair and skin are so white he almost seems to lack any color at all, and yet, his features are as intensely beautiful as almost anyone I've seen. Perhaps even more so, given the nearly palpable aura of his confidence.

If I wasn't sure that I had already heard him speak, I might think he was a marble statue carved by the gods themselves.

His gaze travels slowly over the room, taking in the creatures as they seek their pleasure from one another. The light pouring in from above frames him in a golden glow as he lounges there, content simply to watch.

A grin tugs at the corner of his mouth as he revels in the intimate chaos that fills the room before his eyes finally settle on us.

Slowly, he sits up before leaning forward to brace his forearms on his knees, his head cocking slightly to one side. His brow arches as he takes in Persephone before his eyes shift to me.

I suddenly feel naked, a blush rising to my cheeks as he almost seems to see straight into the very depths of my being.

"There is no Anteros here," he says, his voice melting over me. Again, despite my best efforts, I find myself leaning forward as I hang off of every word he says.

He grins rakishly, his eyes never leaving me. I wait with bated breath to hear what he'll say next, despite the embarrassment that floods through me at this.

"It is only I, *Eros*, God of Lust and Desire."

12

DEATH

I glance down at Persephone, furious at her for this, only to realize from her own reaction that she did not mean for this encounter. She seems just as disturbed to find Eros here as I am.

"Eros, what are you doing here?" she asks. "Where is your brother?"

Eros grins, and I hate how even I am not completely immune to his charm.

I feel the draw of his power. Notice his every move, his every word, and his every look. There is a certain appeal to him that I cannot ignore, and I must be wary of it for Hazel's sake.

Especially when I see the way he looks at her, hunger practically making his skin glow, and he does not even know what she is yet.

If I am not careful, she will be unable to resist him, mortal as she is.

After all, he is lust, desire ... *sex* incarnate.

I can feel the way he is feeding off the very energy of

the creatures in this room, draining them of their desires in order to satiate himself.

"We made a temporary switch," Eros explains coolly. "I am allowing Anteros the benefits of ... certain aspects of my own palace as a wedding gift. Funny, is it not, how age-old feuds seem to all but disappear when desire comes into play?"

Persephone lets out an annoyed huff before glancing up at me.

"I swear I did not know," she says. "Had I, I would never have brought you here."

"I know," I say. "Come, let us be gone from here."

"What, and ruin the fun?" Eros exclaims as he rises to his feet, once more demanding our attention with the lure of his voice.

He takes his time sauntering off the dais on which Anteros' throne sits. Moving through the creatures, they reach for him, crying out as they try to get him to join them. But he ignores their pleas, his sights set on us.

Even in his refusal, though, his mere proximity is enough to help heighten their passion and ecstasy, their sighs and moans intensifying as he passes.

I tense as he approaches, my shadows swirling up around me as I try to block him from sensing Hazel. The last thing that I need right now is for Eros to become interested in her and learn that she is mortal.

I have heard far too many stories about Eros' exploits in the mortal realm to risk that.

I can only hope that Persephone and I are enough of a distraction for him.

"Tell me, why do you seek my brother?" Eros asks.

Persephone opens her mouth to answer, but I cut her off with a look before replying, "That is none of your concern, Eros. My business is with Anteros, not you."

"*Your* business," he says, and I immediately realize that I have said the wrong thing as Eros' pale eyes shift to me. His gaze almost seems to sharpen, despite the fact I know he cannot actually see me.

"We really must be going—" Persephone starts, but Eros holds up a hand to silence her.

"*Your* business," he says again, tilting his head to one side and giving me a grin that does nothing to diminish the way his eyes flash with sudden understanding. In a breath, he steps closer to me, too close for comfort with Hazel tucked just behind me. "Who is she then? The one you shield behind you."

When I do not answer, his eyes shift to Persephone. Turning toward her, he dips his chin, his expression intensifying on her.

"Eros, please," she breathes.

She blushes deeply, biting her lip to the point of drawing blood as she tries her best to resist his charms.

"Fine, if neither of you will tell me, I will ask her myself," he says. Lifting his chin to the air, Eros closes his eyes as he spreads his hands out to either side in dramatic fashion.

My hand on Hazel involuntarily tightens as I clench my teeth together. I can almost feel the way his other senses suddenly heighten, the atmosphere shifting around him.

"Eros," I warn in a low voice.

"Strange," he mutters, ignoring me as his brow

furrows in thought, "I have not met this one here before. She has a certain ... innocence to her that one does not often find among our kind. If ever."

"Which is exactly why you need to let us leave," I say darkly.

Eros' sharp eyes snap open to land on me, and I can see the spark of desire swirling deep within his gaze.

He wants Hazel, or at least the challenge of claiming her.

"Show her to me," Eros demands, stepping closer. "I must know who this creature is that has Death himself wrapped around her finger."

"Do not force me to remind you of your place, Eros," I growl, even as Persephone's eyes widen, and she shakes her head at me. "*I* do not have to bend to the will of lesser gods."

Eros ignores me as he takes another step closer, his eyes never leaving mine. A self-satisfied smirk breaks across his face as he seems to enjoy taunting me.

"I think you have forgotten, Death," he says, "this is currently *my* domain. Making me no lesser of a god than you, or has it really been that long since you were last here?"

"What are you talking about?"

Eros pauses, his brow furrowing in confusion.

"Persephone, did you not tell him?"

"Tell me what?" I ask, glancing between them.

"I must admit, I was surprised when you walked through my doors," he says, my eyes narrowing on him. "Hades was none too pleased after your last visit to the city, and we have all paid dearly because of it."

"What Hades does here is none of my concern."

"Oh, but it is," Eros scoffs, "because, you see, he made a deal with the Fates." A sudden pit forms in my stomach at this, but I do not allow myself to react as I wait for him to continue. "A deal in which, within the walls of Aglaia, *you* are no longer the most powerful being ... and within *these* walls, *I* am your god."

Eros snaps his fingers, and two large beasts suddenly stalk forward to grab me before I have a chance to react. They drag me aside, leaving Hazel exposed to the God of Lust.

"Eros! What is the meaning of this?" I shout, struggling against the grip of the creatures holding me, but to seemingly no avail.

"Death," Hazel cries out just as Eros closes the distance between them and reaches for her.

"No!" I roar, my heart stopping in my chest as his fingertips brush against her skin, and her body stills as she immediately turns to him.

Fear tears its way through me as I wait for any sign that his power has taken hold of her. That he has managed to steal her from me with a single touch.

But her expression remains unreadable, her body unmoving as Eros' hands slowly trace the features of her face.

Jealousy twists at my gut as I watch, and then I see it.

However, instead of Hazel, it is Eros who changes.

His hands still cupped to her face; he blinks. In an instant, his demeanor changes as he glances over at me. I watch as he tries to mask it, but it is already too late.

He is taken with her.

Reflected back at me is an emotion I have come to know far too well, and there is nothing I can do to change it.

Eros is falling for her ... if he has not already. With nothing more than a single touch, I know that he has become intimate with her soul and the depths of her being ... and my heart shatters at the realization that I may no longer be the only one here who loves her.

And yet, I am the only one who cannot give her the affection she so greatly deserves.

The only one who cannot touch her.

13

HAZEL

Up close, Eros is even more striking than I thought.

His face is all sharp angles, only softened by the slight upward turn of his lips; his eyes, framed in thick white lashes, soul-piercing in their paleness. Despite the near translucence of his skin, I can see a smattering of silver freckles across his cheeks and nose, matching the heavy rings adorning his fingers as he leans closer in.

His robes drape over his body, tied loosely at the waist as if they might slip from his shoulders at any moment. Somehow, they manage to reveal just enough of his form to leave you thirsting to see what lies beneath.

I blush at this thought, ashamed to realize my eyes have dipped to trace his lines ever lower. Quickly lifting my eyes, I return them to his face.

Eros towers over me, though not nearly as much as Death does, and has to bend as he takes my face in his hand. I inhale sharply at the heat of his touch, his intoxicating scent crashing over me and filling me with a strange sense of longing.

He's surprisingly gentle, and tender in a way I wouldn't have expected the God of Lust to be familiar with. And yet, it is hard to miss the way he oozes desire and lust.

As his fingers linger on my cheek, though, Eros' expression gradually changes. His brow furrows slightly, even as the corners of his lips remain turned up in a smile.

"What are you?" he asks, his voice coming out breathless as he lifts both hands to cup either side of my face. "You seem familiar, but I cannot ..."

He trails off, and it is only in this moment that I realize Eros is *actually* blind, his fingertips moving slowly across my skin as if trying to learn every little detail they can about me.

Of course, he would have to rely on his other senses to *see* me. It makes so much more sense now than it did but a moment ago.

While his touch is light, barely more than a whisper of his skin against mine, it almost seems to bleed me of myself ... while at the same time igniting a smoldering fire deep within me.

I find myself torn between wanting to give in to it and wanting to pull away. My mind begs me to put as much distance as possible between us, but then some other, primal, part of me cries out for his touch, welcoming it as if I were long craved for affection.

Eros cups the side of my head as his other hand slips

lower, his fingers trailing over the delicate skin as sparks shoot through my body.

Our eyes meet, and though I know he's blind, I swear his sight pierces me to the depths of my being. As if he can see the very essence of who I am.

Suddenly, he bends, his lips parting as he pulls me closer, running a hand through my hair. I don't have time to react, my breath catching in my throat before his mouth finds mine. Eros' kiss is passionate, desperate, and full of longing as if he were trying to consume me with it ... and succeeding.

My heart races, my skin tingling from the heat of his touch as my mind spins in confusion. I feel like I'm drowning, losing myself with each passing second.

The next thing I know, Eros is thrown back from me amidst a sudden flurry of shrieks and screams from the creatures around us.

I collapse to my knees, my body weak and trembling. Gasping, I try to regain my composure as I watch him writhe on the floor, shadows licking their way up his body to wrap around his neck.

"Death, no!" Persephone cries out, but Death ignores her as he stalks toward Eros.

"How *dare* you touch her like that," Death roars, the beasts that were previously restraining him scurrying away in terror as he raises a gloved hand to signal for his shadows to tighten.

For a moment, all I can do is stare in shock and horror at the scene unfolding before me. Blinking, I regain control of my tongue as I reach forward to lay a gentle hand on Death's leg.

"Please," I say softly, forcing my eyes away from Eros as I look up at him. "Please, don't do this."

I see a flicker of what looks like pain in Death's eyes as he glances down at me, but then he blinks and drops his hand. Quickly turning to kneel before me, he grabs my arms and helps lift me back onto my feet. Instantly, his shadows return to him, leaving Eros gasping for air on the marbled floor.

Persephone quickly moves to Eros' side, dropping to her knees to check on him as Death searches my face.

"I am sorry, little one," he says after a quiet moment. "I ... We should leave this place at once."

He pulls me to his side, slipping a hand around my waist for support, before turning toward the door just as Eros pushes himself up onto his elbows.

"You cannot leave," he says, his chest still heaving.

"Do not make me—"

"She is mortal," Eros interrupts. "Her soul, you are going to need my help to save it."

Death freezes, his shoulders tensing as he slowly turns us back to look at the pale god.

"I need no one's help, especially not when it comes from the likes of you."

Eros lets out an unsettling laugh at this, waving away Persephone's offered hand as he rises to his feet.

"You are going to need all the help you can get, if I am not mistaken as to why you came here," he says, his white eyes slowly lifting to meet Death's as he rubs his neck. "Besides, it was not an offer. It was a statement. You came for my brother's help; take mine in his stead."

"No."

"Death," Persephone says, stepping nervously toward us, "he is not wrong about needing help. You do not know—"

"I said no," Death snarls, his hand tightening around my waist. "Of all the gods I trust least, he is among the worst."

My heart pounds as I look glance between them, tension filling the room as the creatures around us give up all pretense of minding their own business.

"I think we should hear what he has to offer," I say, the words slipping from me before I can stop them.

Death looks away, obviously disliking the idea, before letting out a deep sigh.

"Fine, what is it that you suggest?" he asks, his voice hard as his eyes darken on Eros.

"Well, first, I need to know exactly what you were seeking my brother's help with."

"I thought you said—"

"Cerberus," Persephone answers, cutting Death off. "We need help convincing him to betray Hades, *temporarily*, in favor of letting Hazel escape the underworld."

Eros doesn't say anything for a moment as he furrows his brow in thought. Death continues to stare at him, his shadows curling up around us in icy waves, and I wonder if I've made a mistake asking him to listen.

Suddenly, Eros straightens, a grin spreading across his face as he looks at each of us excitedly.

"I know exactly how I can help," he says. "I will help the mortal seduce Cerberus."

"Absolutely not," Death growls, an angry snort fluttering the fabric of his mask slightly. "Come, Hazel."

"I am the God of Lust and Desire, am I not?" Eros calls out as Death turns to drag me out of the room. "What better way is there to win someone over to your side than to offer them what they most desire?"

Death keeps his eyes trained forward, his chin dropping slightly as he ignores him.

"Wait," Persephone says as she hurries to follow at our side. "This could work. It is not what I originally planned, but it may be exactly what you need."

"No."

"It might even be the fastest way, the safest way of ensuring you get out of here in time."

"I said, no," Death snaps, his black eyes widening with rage as he turns on her. "I will not allow it. It is far too dangerous."

"For her ... or you?" Persephone asks quietly, stopping Death in his tracks. He looks away, his jaw working beneath his mask as if he's trying to maintain his composure. "Death, this may very well be your only option. Hades has turned many against you since last you were here. You cannot be certain that anyone else will help."

"And that is supposed to make me willing to entrust her to *him*?"

I glance between them, confusion worrying my brow as I think about everything that's been said. Wouldn't it just be easier to toss Cerberus a steak or two to win him over rather than try to seduce him?

"Wait, I don't understand," I say. "Isn't Cerberus a

dog? Or, at least, a dog-like creature? How would this plan even work?"

They stare at me for a second, and it's obvious I must have misunderstood something. Persephone's eyes suddenly widen in understanding, but it's Eros who answers, "You are not wrong, but that is only his beast form. If you play your cards right, If, you allow me to train you ... I have no doubt that you will discover his true form soon enough."

"That will not happen; we will find another way."

"Let *her* decide," Eros says, drawing closer to us. "After all, it is her soul that is at stake here."

Death tenses, but, much to my surprise, he turns to look down at me, his eyebrow raised in question.

"Fine. What do you want to do, Hazel?"

I blink, taken aback that he would even let me choose, given how *clearly* he dislikes Eros' company.

"Do you really think this will work?" I ask Persephone after allowing myself a moment to think.

"I do," she answers. "Cerberus has lacked companionship for far too long. I doubt it would take much to truly win him over."

I chew my lip nervously, doubting myself as I finally come to a decision. Swallowing past the lump in my throat, I let out a deep sigh as I look between them.

"Okay."

"You do not have to do this, little one," Death says in a low whisper as he gently grabs my upper arms and bends to look me in the eye, suddenly seeming like himself again. "I will end this right here and now, if you but say the word."

"Do you have another plan?" I ask before clarifying, "One that doesn't involve mass slaughter."

His silence confirms my thoughts.

"I detest this plan," he says.

"As do I, but it may be the only chance we have. Hades has already refused us, and if we can't win Cerberus to our side ... then what hope do we have?"

"So, is it decided then?" Eros asks.

Straightening, Death and I turn to face him only to find his hand raised before him, a strangely familiar silver substance swirling around his arm. It takes me a second to realize what it reminds me of, and my eyes widen as I glance up at Death in horror.

"What are you doing with my shadow?" he says, his voice terrifyingly soft.

"I warned you that this palace was *my* domain," Eros says. "As part of Hades' deal with the Fates, any power used against us in our own homes gets partially transferred to us. At least, for as long as the offender remains in the Underworld ... Welcome to the new City of Gods."

"Did you know about this?" Death hisses, whirling on Persephone.

"Of course, but I could not say as much," she says, her cheeks flushing in shame. "It was another part of his deal."

"You need not worry, Death," Eros says as he draws closer, the little bit of silver shadow playfully swirling around him. "I do not need your power, nor do I want it."

With that, he plucks the silver shadow from him and tosses it back at Death. Immediately, it turns inky as it merges with the larger pool of darkness that churns at Death's feet.

"Now, shall we get started," Eros says, his eyes dropping to me. "You need not worry, mortal. I am *the* master of seduction; before too long, you will have Hades' lapdog *begging* to be on his knees before you. Of that, I am sure."

14

EROS

"Come," I say as I move toward the doors, turning to walk backward as I motion for them to follow me. "Let me give you a tour of your new home."

Spinning back around, my back now to them, the grin falls from my face as I let fear take hold of my heart.

All it took was a single touch to spell my ruin.

A single touch of her skin and I was able to see her more clearly than I have ever seen anything in my entire life. And, considering that I am blind, that is saying something.

One kiss was all it took for the darkness of my life to be flooded with light and color, and for a moment, a single heartbeat, I was sated in ways I have never been before.

In ways I never knew were possible for me ... and by a *mortal*, of all creatures.

Her soul, her energy is so pure, so ... fiercely intoxicating in its intensity. I find myself suddenly craving *nothing*, no one but her.

I must have her. I must find a way to claim her, to stay Death's hand from taking her from me, if only just for a time. I will not stop until I do.

Until I have known her.

Hell, what I would give to experience that with her. I do not remember the last time I truly *wanted* to lay with another.

Death lets out a low growl as if he can read my thoughts. Though, I suppose it is my aura he can feel; the way I am drowning after just one touch. How desperate I am to taste her again.

Hmm, Death may prove to be a problem in that regard. His desire for the girl is obvious; it rolls off of him in heavy waves. I could sense it the moment he stepped foot in the palace.

From the girl, though, I can sense nothing when it comes to her own desire. I almost hate the glimmer of hope this thought sparks within me. If she does not desire him, then perhaps she can grow to desire me instead.

I know it is a foolish thought.

Something must have happened between them; why else would Death be willing to risk so much for a mortal?

Aside from my own desire for her, my own desperate and aching hunger to *taste* her, she is an enigma. I cannot help but wish that I could see her face and the emotions that cross it, the way words fall from her lips.

For the first time in my life, I am frustrated with my

inability to physically see, if only because I am unable to experience *everything* she has to offer.

I have to force these thoughts from my mind. It does me no good to wallow in what cannot be changed.

Leading them through the halls of my brother's palace, I give them an offhanded tour as we go, unwilling to give them so much as a glimpse into the turmoil that currently haunts me.

As my frustration over my reaction to her grows, I cannot help but try to rationalize the way she has affected me.

Perhaps, it is because I have never known anyone to have such an effect on Death himself that I am so desperate to make her mine. I cannot understand how a mere mortal could bring a being so feared, by men and gods alike, to his knees.

Though, judging by the tension in his energy, only in the most figurative sense.

The more I consider it, the more I realize that I simply need to bed the girl to get her out of my head. To have my fill of her until I am cured of this madness.

I do not yet know how I will go about accomplishing this, with Death hovering over her, but I will. Then, I can return to my senses.

It is one thing for Death to fall for her; I would probably settle for far less if I were him ...

But me?

I snort softly to myself.

The God of Lust does not fall for *anyone*.

Least of all, a mortal girl.

15

HAZEL

I shift closer to Death, walking as close to him as I can, my strength slowly returning to my body. My hand is wrapped around Death's arm in the hopes that my touch will help ease the tension between us, as well as keep me on my feet.

He glances down at me, his dark eyes unreadable, his expression revealing nothing of his emotions. Still, I can sense his unease as Eros guides us through the palace.

It's obvious he and Eros aren't exactly on the best of terms; however, I'm starting to think he isn't exactly on the friendliest of terms with anyone.

"Ah, my brother's favorite courtyard," Eros says as we walk through a small archway. "I once showed four maidens some of the finer things in life on that very bed of flowers."

Death makes a disgusted sound at this, and Persephone rolls her eyes. Eros turns to glance back at me as if searching for my reaction, and I give him a polite smile, suddenly nervous that he can see more than I think.

I dislike the way he boasts of his past conquests, but it seems wrong to have to express as much when he's the one meant to be helping us.

"The gold here comes from my own personal vault," Eros tells us as we enter a large study. "I had it sent over as a wedding present for my dear brother. See, Death, even *he* can find it in himself to enjoy the finer things in life ... From time to time."

Eros continues his tour, showing us room after room filled with opulent treasures and lavish décor, each one followed up by some story or another. Stepping into yet another room, I suddenly have to fight the urge to move away from Death as my eyes widen on a number of large paintings. They're unlike anything I've ever seen. The paintings are strange, and yet, surreally beautiful in the way color and emotion seem to play out on the canvas.

"These paintings, they're stunning," I murmur.

"Do you think so?" Eros says uncertainly, turning to look at me again. "They are from my private collection. I could not bear to part with them when I agreed to lend my palace to Anteros. They were meant to capture some of the happiest moments of my life, but I do not know if they succeeded in doing so."

"I think they have," I say, my eyes taking in the bold strokes of paint as I try to read the story told within them.

"I think it would be best if we were given a chance to rest and prepare for the task ahead," Death says, clearing his throat. "Hazel will also require food before too long."

I'm taken aback by this remark and wonder if it's actually true or not.

"Ah, yes, right this way," our host says with a small

nod. I am reluctant to leave the paintings behind before I've had the chance to admire them properly, but I do ... after making a mental note to try to sneak back here to admire them if I can.

We walk in silence for a few minutes, and I get the distinct impression that Eros is reminiscing over a fond memory as I watch him.

Until he opens his mouth again.

"Speaking of food. It is a shame, Persephone, that you missed my party last year. I had all the best champagne imported from the mortal realm and chocolates as well. Even managed to sneak some strawberries past Cerberus."

"You know very well why I was unable to attend your party," Persephone says.

"Well, you must admit that Midsummer is the best time for a party. *Especially* one of mine."

Persephone snorts at this but remains quiet, and I don't miss the way Eros glances over at me as if he expects me to be impressed. I supposed I should have known better than to think he was actually recalling something meaningful.

The more Eros talks, the less and less I seem to like him, despite the allure of his voice. As beautiful as he is, he lacks depth and is far too full of himself.

I am starting to worry that he may not actually be capable of helping us.

Perhaps trusting him was a mistake. A mistake I can blame on no one but myself but could end up costing us our future.

Chewing my lip nervously, Eros leads us into a vast

greenhouse, and yet again, I find myself looking around in awe. The room is full of life—vibrant sun-kissed petals spill out in every imaginable hue—vines weaving through intricate lattices and overflowing with a profusion of blooms that fill the air with a heady fragrance.

"Oh," Persephone gasps in delight, "Eros, is this your doing?"

"I thought you might like it," he says with a bright grin, surprising me as he glances back at her. "I had to brave the mortal realm in order to gather some of these, and it is a good thing I did. Many of these have gone extinct since I was last there."

My eyes flicker between them, watching as his eyes soften at her delight, and yet again, I question whether I've been too quick to judge Eros. Perhaps there is more to him than meets the eye.

And then, he has to go and ruin everything by opening his mouth again.

"In fact, the last time I was there, I came across some of the most fascinating mortals. The stories I could tell you about my time amongst them ... the *things* I taught them," he boasts, arching his brow at me. "I would not be surprised if they still whisper about them behind closed doors. Not that I ever stooped so low as to join them, of course."

This is met with an uncomfortable silence, and Eros' smile slips.

"Our *rooms*, Eros," Death presses through clenched teeth.

Persephone snorts at this, and I take a step closer to Death. The chill of his body so near to mine is a welcome reminder that we're in this together. That I'm not about to face whatever lies ahead, or Eros, on my own.

My faith in Eros may be wavering, but at least I'm not alone. For that small fact, I'm eternally grateful.

"This way," Eros says, his smug tone suddenly distant.

None of us says a thing as we walk, our footsteps ricocheting off the pearly marble of the halls. Distantly, I can hear the gathering we'd walked in back in full swing, the sounds of pleasure floating through the air making my cheeks burn.

Suddenly, I'm not sure how I'll ever be able to fall asleep in a place like this, and I can't help but miss the dark, quiet halls of Death's palace. Despite how cold it was.

It suddenly dawns on me how comfortable I have been here, even standing so close to Death. The heat of Eros' palace balanced out by Death's chill.

"I am assuming you will not be staying with us, Persephone," Eros says, finally breaking the silence between us as we make our way up several flights of stairs.

"You would be correct," she says.

"Shame. I had hoped you might join us."

"I will be sure to stop by as often as I can," she says, giving Death a knowing look. "Besides, someone has to make sure you actually have the time to prepare."

"How are going planning to go about that?" Eros asks suddenly, turning toward her.

"I will think of something."

"I could give you a young succubus," he offers. "I know a particularly good one who would certainly keep your husband—"

"No," Persephone interrupts, her cheerful demeanor instantly darkening. "I said will handle my husband."

"Suit yourself," he says with a shrug.

Turning down another hall, I find it lined with elegant doors, though they are spread far and few between. My nervousness only seems to grow as I watch Eros' excitement increase with each step and every door he passes.

I tighten my grip on Death, and he pulls me gently closer just as I realize there's only one set of doors left. Eros leads us toward the ornate double doors at the far end of the hall.

"Here we are," Eros says, flashing a bright grin at us all before throwing open the doors.

My eyes widen as I take in the room beyond. The far wall is made entirely of an unusual opalescent glass that looks out over the gardens and city beyond the palace walls. Light filters through it in pastel rainbows that shimmer over gold furniture upholstered in creamy velvets. At the center of the room is a four-poster bed, covered in a plush duvet and golden pillows of various shapes and sizes, complete with a fluttering canopy of soft white.

It's exactly how I would have imagined a bedroom in a god's palace, yet it still, somehow, exceeds my wildest expectations.

"This is where the mortal will stay," Eros says, surprising me.

"No," Death answers without hesitation.

Eros snorts as he turns to stare down Death, and again, I wonder just how much the world he can actually see. Surely, if nothing else, he can sense the sudden surge of fury that is now rolling off Death.

I glance between them and then around the room, wondering what it is exactly that's upset him. Perhaps there is more at play here than I can see.

"She is not staying in *your* bedchamber, Eros," Death growls.

I balk at this realization, understanding Death's displeasure in an instant.

"Why not?" Eros asks.

"Eros—"

"As my guest, does she not deserve the best? Certainly, *you* of all beings cannot expect me to offer her anything less. Give me one good reason why she should not stay in this room, aside from the fact that it is mine."

Eros raises an eyebrow in challenge; the smile playing at the corners of his lips, a taunting one. He's obviously trying to get a reaction from Death, but he remains as cold as ever. Straightening, he stares down at Eros as the light seems to ebb and flow around us, neither wavering in their resolve.

The moment seems to stretch on forever as I finally glance over at Persephone for help, but she simply gives me a small smile and shake of her head.

"You *are* the reason. I know better than to think that you would give up your bed," Death says. "I have sworn to protect her, and that includes from the likes of you."

"You cannot possibly think that I would harm a hair on her head," Eros says with a laugh so low and dangerous that it sends a shiver down my spine. "Do you trust me so little, even after all these years?"

"No. I do not trust you at all," Death replies evenly. "I know your nature, Eros. I know that you will stop at nothing to get what you want, and I will not leave you to have your way with her."

Death's words have an immediate effect on Eros, his grace and careful tone slipping away to reveal a creature far more terrifying. Though still stunningly beautiful, the man standing before us now is no longer dripping in arrogance but fury.

Huge white wings suddenly burst out from Eros' back, and in a breath, the two men have closed the space between them. Death's shadows swirl up around them, the tension in the room soaring to new heights as they stare each other down.

"Is that so?" Eros says, his voice soft and deadly. "And what if I told you that she wants me just as much as I want her?"

I inhale sharply at this, but Death simply narrows his eyes. "I do not believe you."

"Then why not ask her yourself," Eros asks. "Ask your mortal if she would take me, God of Desire, into her bed ... or are you too afraid to find out?"

The leather of Death's glove tightens, and for a breath, I'm sure he's about to launch himself at Eros. But then, the frost chilling the air softens as a warm breeze whips up around us, filling our lungs with an intoxicating, floral scent.

Persephone steps forward, the tension easing just enough to relax my shoulders as she pushes her way between the two men. The tiny goddess presses a palm to each of their chests, forcing them back a step as she frowns up at the two men, anger flashing across her beautiful face. At her touch, Eros' wings fold and disappear, and Death's shadows calm.

"Enough! We do not have time for this," she hisses. "Eros, you are being difficult, and I have little patience left these days for difficult men. Gods or not. Death, Hazel will stay in this room, and that is final."

"Who are you to dictate—"

"She *must*," Persephone snaps, stomping her foot down hard on the marble, a burst of petals floating down around her feet as she glares up at Death.

"And why is that?" he snarls back, his shadows starting to churn at his feet once again.

"Because she will only be safe in my room," Eros interrupts, drawing our attention back to him with the seriousness of his voice, "that is why I offer it."

Death pulls back, his brow furrowing in confusion.

"What do you mean?"

"As long as Hades' deal is in place, no one can set foot in a god's bedchambers without explicit permission," he says.

"The only exception to this rule is if someone's mate is within," Persephone adds.

"And you did not think to start with this information?" Death says. My gaze flickers between them as I try to make sense of these gods and their strange rules. "Still, I will not leave her alone with him."

"Then perhaps a compromise is in order," she sighs, the perfumed air growing heavier around us, "all three of you will share Eros' room."

A moment of quiet passes before Eros lifts his shoulders in a half-shrug, and I realize this is his way of agreeing to her compromise.

Frowning, I glance up at Death. Darkness and frost still seep from him, though it is softened by the warm breeze, as he stares down at the others.

Despite what they've told us, I get the feeling he has no intention of accepting the offer. Quickly stepping forward before Death's anger can return, I place a gentle hand on his arm. Instantly his eyes snap to me, softening as they find my face.

"It is only temporary," I say gently, "and we need all the help we can get. Besides, with you by my side, no harm will come to me."

"Fine," Death says, his shoulders relaxing slightly, "but this does not mean I trust you, Eros."

"Then it seems that we have finally reached an understanding," Eros says with a rakish grin. "Death, welcome to my private chambers."

16

DEATH

All it takes is her hand on my arm.

A single touch and I can feel the icy rage within me thaw for her.

One word from her, and my resolve shatters into a million pieces.

Hazel could ask me to bend my neck to a sword, and I would, without question. She need only ask, and I would do anything, give anything, for her.

And yet, I know these promises are little more than pretty lies. Illusions of selflessness when, in reality, they mean nothing.

I would kneel, but the blade would not kill me. She could ask for my touch, but I would refuse for fear of harming her.

In truth, I am powerless, watching on as another man touches her, invites her into his bed ... and she accepts.

Perhaps I was mistaken about the painting, about the depth of her feelings for me. Perhaps Eros is right about her wanting him, and I am the one too blind to see it.

After all, I am the one who killed her with a kiss she never asked for. Can I truly blame Hazel if she wants someone else?

Someone she can kiss without the threat of death.

My heart hardens again at the memory of their kiss, and I swallow back shame, furious with myself for breaking so easily. I swore to protect her, I should have known better than to come to this city with her, and now ... I have led her straight into the lion's den.

"Good," Persephone says with a clap of her hands, dragging my attention back to her. "I am glad that is settled."

I grimace at her forced cheeriness and note the way she avoids meeting my eye as she takes a step back. I watch her, sensing unease starting to creep in at the edges of her perfumed air.

"Will you be back?" Hazel asks.

"Yes," she says. "As soon as I have news of Cerberus and my husband's plans. Now, I really must be going; I have already been gone far too long as it is."

With that, she hurries away. The moment her colorful skirts disappear around the corner, a chill rushes in to replace her conjured warmth, and I bristle as I turn back to Eros.

We say nothing to each other, and I consider, for the briefest of moments, how satisfying it would be to break his nose. From the way he is looking at me, I have no doubt he feels the same, but then his gaze shifts to Hazel.

"Come, let me show you where everything is," he says, offering his hand to her. "I would like to make sure you have everything you need during your stay with me."

Hazel moves away from me, and I immediately feel the loss of her touch.

"Your room is lovely," she says, walking past his offered hand as she steps further into his bedroom. Perhaps she did not notice it, but this slight has hope taking root in my chest. I know better than to believe that she is completely immune to Eros' charms, but perhaps she is not as easily swayed by them as I thought.

I see the way Eros is drawn to her ... *feel* the way he seems unable to stop searching the room for her, despite his supposed distaste for lesser mortal souls.

Trailing behind them, I watch as he follows her, and she shifts slightly away each time he steps too close. I cannot help the faintest of smiles from tugging at my lips at the way she interacts with him.

Is it possible that I was wrong? Is she not affected by Eros' power at all?

It seems too good to hope for. Perhaps she simply means not to offend me by throwing herself at him, but even that would suggest his charms do not hold as much power over her as they should.

Either way, I have no intention of letting her out of my sights. Especially not with him at her side. He is a danger to her, even if neither of them sees the other in that way.

I know far too much about Eros' past. I have seen the way men and women alike have tossed themselves at his feet, only to be cast aside, their bodies and souls drained and broken. I will not allow that to happen to Hazel.

My gaze follows the two of them about the room, my body ready to act at a moment's notice, should I need to.

Hazel nods and smiles politely as Eros shows her every little detail of the room.

It seems unnecessary, but I resist the urge to step in. Hazel moves to stand in front of the windowed wall, Eros stepping into place behind her, and I watch as he moves to place his hand on the small of her back.

I see black, my fists clenching as my shadows stir, waiting for my command, but I am saved from action by a servant suddenly appearing at the door.

"My lord," the creature says, glancing warily at me, "there is someone here to meet with you. I told him to wait in the main courtyard."

"Ah, it seems that duty calls," Eros says, returning Hazel to my side. "I am afraid we must part ways for now. I will be sure to send someone to escort you to dinner before too long."

Eros gives me a look before motioning for the servant to lead the way, closing the doors behind him.

Silence fills the space where he once was, and I almost let out a sigh of relief to finally have him gone. To finally have a few moments alone with Hazel and away from prying eyes and ears.

"I—"

"How—" Hazel says at the same time, and we both pause. She lets out a small laugh, teasing a smile to my lips as our eyes meet.

"You first, little one," I say as she glances away, her cheeks flushing.

"How ..." she starts hesitantly. "How exactly do you think Eros plans on teaching me?"

The smile slips from my face, though hidden behind

my mask, and a sigh of frustration escapes me before I can stop it. Hazel looks up, her brow worried with concern, patiently waiting for me to answer as I try my best to temper my displeasure over the thought first.

If I know anything about Eros, and I do, I can only begin to imagine what he plans to do with her. This thought alone is more than enough to tempt me into tracking him down and ending whatever tentative peace we have established.

After allowing myself a moment to contemplate what I would do to him, I realize that Hazel is still waiting for an answer.

"I cannot say for sure," I admit, "but I believe he will try to teach you his *art* by trying to perform it on you."

"Oh," she gasps, her cheeks warming, as she looks away again.

"What did you expect, little one?"

"I don't know, but ... do you really think he would waste his powers on me? I am nothing but a mortal; surely, he would prefer to show me what to do with a more suitable partner?"

She shakes her head, and I watch as she struggles to overcome her surprise. Part of me wants to believe she is now regretting her decision to accept his help, but another part of me worries that she is enticed by the idea.

So, I refrain from asking.

"You are so far from being nothing, Hazel," I say, reaching out to lift her chin with the edge of a finger. "Here, amongst these demons, you are *everything*. You are a light amidst and endless world of darkness, and we but dark moths to your flame. Eros would be lucky to have you."

I grimace as I say this, but I cannot deny the truth in them. He would be lucky, if he does not end up dead first.

"You flatter me," she says with a snort of disbelief. "I know the life I led before, and I—"

"No, I simply speak the truth. Think of your father," I say firmly, my heart swelling with affection and admiration for her. "Think of him, of what you gave up to save him. You have already proven the great worth of your soul, and Eros would be a fool not to see it."

Again, I hate myself for bringing up his name, but I cannot allow her to think *she* is the one not worthy of *him*.

Hazel says nothing to this. Her brow furrows as she looks up at me for a moment before gently pulling away from my grip.

I am reluctant to let her go, but I have no choice.

She moves several steps away, turning so that her back is to me, and I am unable to make out any of her emotions as I stare at her. Slowly, she turns back to look at me, her large eyes soft as they search my face.

"Sydian, I want y—" she starts just as the doors to the room are thrown open.

Infuriated, I turn toward them, expecting to find Eros standing before me to ruin things once more.

Except it is not him. Two succubae stand at the threshold, their expressions nervous as they glance at me before quickly dropping their eyes to the floor.

"You're to change and meet Eros for dinner," one of the females says, her eyes slowly lifting to look up at me through heavy lashes, a smirk on her lips.

So, this is the game Eros wants to play? Unfortunately for him, I have little interest in the dark creatures of his court and their wicked charms.

"And we have been instructed to help," the other says as they both step into the room. My eyes narrow on them, taking in the garments draped over their arms, and I let out a sigh.

"Very well, let us get this over with," I say, knowing full well these creatures have been sent to spy on us in Eros' absence, and my moment alone with Hazel has passed.

17

HAZEL

Two of the most beautiful women I have ever seen step into the room, and I watch as they hungrily eye Death before one of them moves toward me.

"Let's get you cleaned up," she says, glancing over her shoulder at Death and her companion as she takes my arm and drags me toward another door.

I look back just as the other woman leads Death behind a dressing partition on the opposite side of the room.

For a split second, I feel a sickening sense of jealousy settle in the pit of my stomach as I imagine the strange woman watching Death undress. Pushing this thought aside, I try to focus on the task at hand as I'm pulled into a private bathroom.

The woman busies herself with drawing a bath, the steam soon filling the spacious room. I warily watch as she pours several jars of something into the water before turning to beckon me over. I eye her, wondering if I can really trust her after seeing the effect Eros seems to have on those around him.

"Come, now, I won't bite," the woman says, flashing a sharp-toothed grin at me.

Walking cautiously toward the bath, I am suddenly hit by an overwhelmingly calming scent and find myself relaxing slightly. I glance down at the water to find it's now glimmering a soft purple, and I can't help but stare at it.

The woman rises, and I tense as she moves toward me. It takes me a moment to realize she means to undress me before I quickly take a step back.

"I can undress myself, thank you."

She blinks, obviously taken aback by this, as I remove my boots and turn to start unlacing myself. I can still feel her eyes on me as the dress loosens around me, and I nervously glance back at her.

"Would you mind looking away?" I ask, hating the way my voice barely makes it past my lips.

Her head tilts slightly to one side, obviously finding my request strange, but then she does as I've asked and turns her back to me. I fight back a sigh of relief as I allow my dress to fall and pool around my feet, a small cloud of dust curling up as it hits the floor.

I'm surprised to see it and am instantly reminded of my days back home, where I was no stranger to being covered in dirt and, often, much worse. I find it odd how the Underworld seems to have so many similarities to the mortal realm.

Especially when it comes to things like this.

Before I let this thought consume me, I quickly turn

and, making sure the woman's back is still to me, lower myself into the bath. Immediately, the sigh of relief I've been biting back escapes me as the hot water welcomes me.

Whatever the woman poured into the tub seems to ease the weariness of travel, wrapping me in a soft blanket of serenity as I close my eyes and sink lower in the water, savoring the moment.

A moment that is over in an instant as a cold hand touches my shoulder. I let out a startled scream as I turn and scramble back from the edge of the tub. My eyes wide as I find the woman knelt, one hand caught between us as the other holds a sponge.

She only meant to wash me, I realize in embarrassment as my heart starts to settle in my chest. However, before I can say anything, the door to the room slams open, startling me all over again as I quickly wrap my arms around myself.

Death stands in the doorway, half-dressed, his shoulders pulled back, and his fists clenched as his eyes dart around the room. He's still wearing his makeshift mask, but it does little to conceal his rage as his shadows crash around him, framing the icy paleness of his bare chest in their fury. Black lines etch their way up his arms and torso, matching the inky shadows at his command.

"What happened?" he demands, his eyes finding me.

"Nothing, I was just startled, that's all," I answer quietly, my gaze dipping lower only to catch on the markings of an animal bite on his arm.

My voice has him drawing back slightly, his eyes softening as his shadows slowly pool at his feet. As he finally regains his composure, he clears his throat as it suddenly hits him that he's staring at me naked in the tub. Blinking, he quickly drops his gaze, realizing the delicate situation we've found ourselves in.

"I-I apologize," he says quickly, turning his back to me, "please, forgive me for my intrusion."

Before I have a chance to answer, let alone ask him about the bite, he strides from the room and closes the door softly behind him. If I didn't know better, I'd almost think he was more embarrassed that he'd walked in on me naked than I was at being seen.

My cheeks burn with heat as I sink lower in the water. I can't help the way my mind wanders to the sight of him bursting in, his powerful chest heaving, ready to protect me at a moment's notice.

It did something to me, ignited an unquenchable fire deep within me that has left me wanting.

Wanting *him*.

As beautiful as the other gods are, even they don't measure up to the perfection that is Death. Seeing him standing there, I could hardly believe that concealed beneath layers of heavy black clothing, is an even more beautiful man than I ever could have imagined.

Suddenly, I wonder how much he saw of me. I had done my best to cover myself, but that doesn't mean he didn't see anything ...

What if he didn't like what he saw?

I know this should be the least of my concerns, but I can't help worrying. I know my time back home, with Merelda's endless chores and lack of proper meals, did me no services. I know I lack the kind of curves I saw among the women in Eros' throne room, or even the two here with us now ... Not even a month at Death's could remedy what years of malnourishment had done to my figure.

It was one thing for him to see me in a dress, quite another to see what I lacked in beauty beneath. Especially in comparison to him.

I glance at the woman meant to be helping me bathe as she leans against the edge of the tub, swirling one finger in the water out of boredom. Even she is a thousand times more beautiful than I could ever hope to be.

She, or her companion, is more likely to capture Death's attention.

Not me.

With a frustrated sigh, I force these thoughts from my mind before I can spiral any further.

In reality, it matters little what he saw or whether he was disappointed or not. I feel ridiculous for even having these thoughts.

Of course, he doesn't see me in that way. Our kiss was little more than a moment of weakness in an ocean of overwhelming emotions.

He made that obvious when he mentioned how he thinks Eros plans to help us. How he means to *let* him train me, despite his initial reaction in the throne room.

I shudder at the thought.

If he truly loved me, surely, he would have told me by now.

No, I am little more than a fly caught in his web of guilt. I should have known better than to hope for more.

To *want* more.

With a sigh, I slip beneath the water in an attempt to drown the thoughts from my mind. I need to focus on the task at hand. I need to remember that I no longer have a promised future.

Death was right; I need to think of my father.

I need to focus on returning to my body ... and, hopefully, making something of my life. To pick up the pieces and move on. I want to see Father again, to feel his arms around me once again.

To I want to forge a future that we would both be proud of.

Though I do not know how I will do that if I am still blamed for Amadeus' death. I frown, realizing a return to the mortal realm may not be as simple as I thought ... and I wonder if it's a life I even want anymore.

18

HAZEL

I allow myself to soak in silence for several minutes longer before turning to the woman meant to be helping me.

"I'm sorry about earlier," I say, her gaze suddenly sharpening as she glances up at me. "I—"

"Are you ready to let me help then?" she asks, startling me with the abruptness of her question.

"You really don't have to. I'm used to taking care of myself." She lets out a huff at this, sinking down again to lean against the edge of the tub in boredom. "I mean ... unless you want to?"

She sits up again, her eyes bright again.

"Of course, I want to," she answers, splashing the space in front of her. "Come."

I do as she bids, and she sets to work scrubbing me down. Unlike Merelda, her touch is gentle, almost erotic, in its thoroughness. I blush as she gushes over me, complimenting the softness of my skin, the rosiness of my cheeks, the warmth of my body.

I murmur my thanks but soon find it overwhelming as she finds more and more ways to flatter me. Tuning her out as she moves on to washing my hair, I decide this must be part of her job. I can almost hear Eros demanding it, insisting that those who serve him feed his ravenous ego.

It's strange to have her hands on my scalp, massaging scented oils into my hair as they lull me into a sense of calm. When she's finally satisfied with my cleanliness, she helps me stand before wrapping me in a soft towel.

Leading me across the room, she sets me down on a small stool beside a fire that burns with iridescent flames. As I watch it, she sets to work on my hair with a silver comb. The woman runs it deftly through my hair, detangling it without pain before braiding it into an intricate pattern around my head.

She hums a soft tune while she works, and I drift along with it. As warmth washes over me, I find it strange to think that my body lies elsewhere. That I am but a soul torn from its anchor, struggling not to be lost at sea before it can be tethered to safety once more.

Glancing at the fire, I let myself get lost watching the flames dance and am reminded of the first time I woke in Death's palace. It isn't long before happy memories of my time in his palace replace the rest.

"When you are ready, I've lain out your dress," the woman tells me, her voice lyrical as she backs away from me.

Dragging myself away from the fire, she leads me over to the dress she's arranged on one counter. I stare at it for a long moment, unable to comprehend how it could possibly be for me. The white fabric is stunning, soft and airy, and unlike any garment that I have ever seen.

I have absolutely no idea how I am supposed to put it on, let alone if it's something I should wear at all.

"These first."

The woman reaches for a set of undergarments next to the dress, presenting them to me. I stare at the tiny gold pieces of fabric, my cheeks burning with heat as I realize they'll most likely be seen through the sheer silk of the dress.

"I don't think I can wear this."

"Nonsense, Eros chose this himself," she says. "Don't worry, I will assist you. It is a rather complicated piece."

I decide to give it a chance before deciding anything and quickly slip on the strange undergarments as she reaches for my towel. She helps me wrap the long gold threads around my body, securing them in place before slipping the dress over my head.

Instantly, I know I never would have figured out how to wear it without her help. As she finishes arranging it over my body, she pins it in place. Stepping back, her eyes sparkle as she gives me an approving nod.

I'm almost nervous to glance toward one of the large mirrors, but I do as curiosity wins out. The dress plunges nearly to my navel, the soft curve of my breasts just barely exposed as long slits ride high up over my hips, exposing the length of my legs with even the smallest of movements.

Surprisingly, though I can see glimpses of the gold undergarments beneath, the white fabric is wrapped in such a way that it is more alluring than it is revealing.

At least, compared to what I thought it would be, as this is still by far the most exposed that I have ever been while somehow being considered fully dressed.

"Don't you think it's a little much?" I ask.

"No, you look beautiful," she says, stepping toward me and turning me away from the mirror. She reaches up to undo several of the braids, allowing some of my hair to cascade down my back in soft waves before giving me one last nod. "And now, you look perfect."

Before I can turn to see the finished look, there's a knock at the door, and my attendant moves to open it, revealing her companion on the other side.

"Eros has summoned them for dinner," she says.

I'm ushered from the bathroom and into the center of the room to find a small man waiting just outside the bedroom door.

"I am here to escort you and your companion to dinner," he says with a small nod toward me.

"Where is Death—"

My heart skips a beat in my chest as I hear the soft clearing of a throat behind me. Turning, I find Death standing before me.

He looks as handsome as ever in an all-black outfit and a brand-new skull mask. I'm both amazed and confused by how perfectly it fits him, both seeming to cover him in his entirety and yet, accentuate every powerful line of his body.

I can't help the way my eyes move to take all of him in, blushing as I see that the fabric leaves the shape of him more exposed to me than I had previously realized. My body has already sparked to life as I quickly drag my eyes back to his, only to find his own still searching me.

It seems neither of us is able to summon the words to voice our amazement. At least, that's what I secretly hope is causing his silence.

Pulling myself together, I search my mind desperately for something to say before I find myself lost in him again.

"You look," I pause, allowing my eyes to take him once again before giving him a small smile, "absolutely terrifying."

My words elicit a spark within his gaze, his shadows dancing up around him. In response, his eyes drop to rake over my body once more. I feel heat burning through me as he takes his time, letting his eyes trail over my curves. As the seconds pass, I find myself unable to stop tugging at the dress, fearing that he will consider it too revealing. Too inappropriate for someone like me.

"Do you not like it?" I ask, anxiety getting the better of me.

"No," Death answers, his voice so low it sends a chill racing down my spine. "You look ravishing, as always, little one. It is only that, seeing you dressed like that and in a place like this, I fear my patience, as well as my self-control, will be tested. I have no doubt all eyes will be on you tonight."

"I can ask to change—" I start, looking down at myself worriedly.

"Absolutely not," he growls, stepping closer to tilt my chin toward him. "As long as you are happy in it, I would have them look ... and I will make them bleed for you, if necessary."

My heart races in my chest at this, my mouth having gone dry at his words. Perhaps I was wrong; perhaps there is still a spark between us just waiting to be set ablaze.

Death runs his gloved thumb over my chin before stepping back to offer me his arm. I take it without hesitation, thankful for the distraction, as we turn toward the man waiting in the doorway.

We follow him in silence, moving through the marbled halls that seem to almost whisper in anticipation of the night ahead. However, the further we walk, the more anxious I become over the thought of joining Eros and his court for dinner.

Death's words echo through me, and I worry that he will be proven correct. That all eyes will be on me, a mere mortal, and I will be found wanting.

I cling tighter to Death's arm as we finally step into a lush hanging garden. Twinkling lights dance between pastel flowers that lightly scent the soft breeze. Cushions have been spread out on the grass, with several low tables between them.

My eyes catch on the food that is piled high on each of the tables. I can't even begin to name half of it as my stomach gives a soft growl, reminding me it's been days since I last ate.

Death tucks me closer to his side as we step into view of the others as they mill about the sprawling garden. Several turn to us, raising crystal goblets in silent greeting, and I blush as one of them gives me an appreciative once-over.

We barely make it more than a few steps, though, before Eros suddenly appears, a grin spreading across his face as he takes us in. Around him, several stunning women shift toward him as if instantly drawn to his presence.

He ignores them, even as some of the braver ones reach to grab at the lengths of his white garments. Eros shakes them off with ease, though the desire in their eyes remains hungry as they continue to stare at him.

"Welcome," he says in greeting. "I am happy to see you both have accepted my small gift of new clothing. I must say, your presence is ... enchanting in it."

Eros directs this last part toward me, reaching out to take my free hand before I can protest and bringing it to his lips. Death tenses as Eros presses a kiss to the back of my hand and gives me a brilliant smile.

I try my best to force a smile of my own onto my lips, even as his touch seems to drain me from the very depths of my being, and I debate how best to politely steal my hand back.

"Thank you," I say, curious how he knows how I look. Even now, as he stares at me with his white eyes, they appear unfocused. Surely, he can't *actually* see what we are wearing and is just giving me a compliment in the hopes of winning me over.

Still, I'm unsettled by the fact that I have no idea how much he sees, and I make a mental note to ask Death if he knows.

"Come, let us feast," Eros says.

With my hand still in his, and my strength slowly draining from me, I have little choice but to trail after him as he turns. Death allows my arm to slip from his, but catches my hand instead as Eros drags me behind him, weaving his way through those gathered about the garden.

Several nod and smile at him, though he makes no show of seeing them. Suddenly, Eros gives me a small tug as he abruptly changes directions, and my hand slips from Death's before he can catch it.

Thankfully, we come to a stop at a crowded table, piled high with delicious-smelling food, the next second.

"Leave us," Eros says, waving his free hand at those seated around the table.

They glance between us, sharing knowing smiles and small looks between them, before doing as Eros demands. Surprisingly, they don't appear too put out over losing their seats to us.

Eros grins at me as he flops down atop the cushions, pulling me down on top of him in the process. I collapse onto the cushions next to him in a far less graceful heap, praying that my dress is still held together as I finally manage to untangle myself from him.

Death settles on the cushions opposite us, his eyes checking in on me before narrowing on Eros.

"You must be famished," he says, reaching across to a pile of plums and plucking one to place on the empty plate in front of me.

"Thank you."

"I always find that when I travel, even the smallest of distances, I am always ready for a good meal," he says, adding a leg of some unknown meat and a handful of spiced almonds to my plate. "The last time I went to a party, I was absolutely appalled that they offered their guests no refreshments. Imagine."

He chatters on, oblivious to Death's glare or the way I don't touch any of the food he continues to add to my plate. My stomach growls, but I find myself suddenly unable to eat, his words barely registering as I take a moment to glance about the garden.

Guests laugh as they eat and sip from their goblets, the heady wine combining with the floral scent of the garden in a way that makes my head spin.

"You must try this," Eros says, pulling my attention back to him as he lifts a goblet full of shimmering liquid to my lips. "Ambrosia of my own making; no mortal has yet tasted it."

Before I can take a sip, Death reaches across the table and places his palm over the goblet. He pushes it back down to the table, his eyes darkening as Eros finally looks his way.

"That is enough, Eros," Death says. "How do you plan to help us deal with Cerberus?"

Eros lets out a sigh. Brushing away Death's hand, he lifts the goblet to his own mouth and drinks deeply from it before setting it back down. His mood suddenly serious as he looks at Death again.

For the first time since sitting, I actually find myself leaning toward him, eager to hear what his plans actually are.

"I suppose that would depend on the mortal," he says, turning to look my way. "Tell me, how much experience do you already have?"

I frown in confusion at his question.

"Experience? In what exactly?" I ask.

"Come, now, there is no need to be coy with me," he snorts. "Nothing you could say would surprise me. Now, tell me, how many men have you invited into your bed?"

Heat floods my body, a wave of shock and embarrassment crashing over me as his question settles on me. My mouth opens, but no words come out.

I am unsure how best to answer him without drawing further humiliation to myself. After several failed attempts, I finally clear my throat and manage to whisper an answer, "None."

The garden falls silent, as if my whispered answer were screamed from the rooftops instead. I draw back as I feel eyes turning toward me, sensing their scrutiny as they stare at me.

Eros is strangely quiet for a moment, and I can't bring myself to meet his gaze.

Or that of Death's.

Instead, I stare at the overflowing plate before me, my stomach knotting within me.

"No one?" Eros finally asks, his voice coming out slightly strained.

I nod, keeping my gaze trained on the table.

Another moment of uncomfortable silence passes, and I have no choice but to glance up.

Eros looks shocked, his eyes wide and mouth slightly agape as he continues to stare at me before turning toward Death.

"I can hardly believe it," Eros admits. "A *virgin* mortal soul. Did you know this about her, Death?"

"No," Death admits. "I did not think it necessary to ask."

"Well, no, I suppose you would not think that. Normally, I would not either, but in this case ..." He pauses before suddenly clapping his hands together, startling me as he continues, "this is excellent news. You, my dear mortal, are a blank canvas. Ready and very willing, I should hope, to be painted with all the colors of desire. Cerberus will not stand a chance against you."

"Does this mean you are ready to share your plan with us?" Death asks.

Eros snorts softly as he shakes his head.

"No," he says. "I need time to digest this new piece of information. For tonight, we must live. Eat, drink, and otherwise enjoy yourselves. Perhaps even you will find a way to partake of the pleasure my court has to offer, Death."

"No," Death says in a low growl of displeasure as he continues to glower at Eros for a moment longer. Around us, the others have returned to their conversations and merrymaking.

"Well, at the very least, the mortal should try to eat something," Eros says. "She will need your strength."

I give Death a questioning look as he lets out a sigh. "He is right. You must eat something, Hazel."

"See?" Eros says with a wink as he reaches across me for a piece of glazed pork and pops it into his mouth.

And just like that, our attention shifts away from my past and our impending future to the revelry at hand.

Hesitantly, I reach for the plum he placed on my plate earlier. The skin gives way to a slight crunch as I bite into it, the sweet tang of the fruit exploding in my mouth as my eyes widen.

I've never tasted a plum so delicious and can't help but smile. Eagerly, I taste the other food, each one as delightful as the last, every bite bursting with flavor.

As amazing as everything is, I am careful to avoid the wine. From what little experience I have with alcohol, I get the impression that ambrosia would be my undoing, and I would much rather keep my wits about me.

Especially around Eros and his guests.

Once everyone has gotten their fill, two beautiful golden-haired women, in green dresses that barely cover anything, stand to make their way across the garden. One of them settles before a golden harp I hadn't noticed before, while the second begins to sing in a voice so stunning it takes my breath away.

It takes less than a minute for the rest of the party to dissolve once more into various stages of lovemaking as soft moans fill the garden. Eros leans back, closing his eyes as if basking in their pleasure.

Unease settles over me as I train my eyes downward in an effort not to watch.

"I believe we should retire," Death says, and a wave of relief washes over me at his suggestion. I don't know how much longer I'd be able to sit here and pretend not to notice what is happening all around me.

"Of course, how thoughtless of me," Eros says. "You must be exhausted."

With a wave of his hand, the man who led us here hurries over and motions for us to follow him.

Death rises before helping me to my feet.

"You are more than welcome to stay, Death. I am sure that even you could find a partner, or two, willing to die for your pleasure ... if you should wish."

"No," he answers coldly before adding, "but, thank you."

I have to fight back a smile as a wave of relief washes over me at his dismissal of Eros' offer. Even if it was a refusal simply because he feels obligated to protect me, I am thankful for it nonetheless.

Though part of me wonders if he's taken Eros up on this offer before, given how quickly it was proffered.

I sneak a glance up at Death, wondering if he could kill someone for the sake of his own pleasure.

"Until morning," Eros calls out in the way of a goodbye, raising his goblet to us as Death leads me away.

19

HADES

"My, my, you have been a busy one, *wife*."

Persephone freezes, her back still to me from where I sit in the dark corner of her room. Slowly, she turns to give me a soft smile.

"Hades, forgive me, I was not expecting the pleasure of—"

"Pleasure," I snort in disgust. "There is no need for such pretenses. There is no pleasure to be found between us. Tell me, where were you today?"

"I was simply taking a stroll through the city. You know how court proceedings can tire me."

"Is that so?" I ask, allowing an edge to creep into my voice. "And if I were to tell you I heard differently?"

"I suppose it would depend on what you heard, as well as who you heard it from."

"Who I heard it does not matter when I have learned that my wife is a traitorous bitch."

Persephone's smile remains plastered to her face, but I can see the fear flicker through her eyes.

"I would never—"

"You would, and you have," I cut her off. "Have I not given you everything? Have I not warned you what would happen if you betrayed me again?"

"Hades, I swear—"

"Lies," I snarl, rising from my chair. Persephone takes a step back, but I close the distance between us with a menacing slowness. "You forget who I am, wife. You forget the power that I hold over you. You forget that I am the God of the Underworld, and that I can make your life more of a living hell than it already is."

Persephone's eyes widen as she stumbles backward. I catch her by her waist, pulling her toward me until there is no space left between us.

I can feel her heart racing against my chest, and I take a moment to relish the fear that I can smell emanating from her skin.

"You forget that I can take away everything you hold dear," I continue, my voice low and dangerous. "So, you will tell me the truth, wife. And you will do it now."

I watch as Persephone's resolve crumbles into tears as she drops her chin, mumbling something that sounds like an apology.

But I do not want her apologies, nor her tears, I want the truth.

"Do not make me force the truth from you, woman," I hiss.

"I ... I was with him."

"With who?" I demand, tightening my grip painfully on her waist.

"Death."

I stare down at her for a long moment before pushing her away from me. She stumbles backward, falling to the ground, and I move to stand over her.

"See? That was not so hard, was it?" I crouch, reaching out to run my hand tenderly over her cheek, brushing away the tears. "I remember a time when we were still in love. A time when you would not dare betray me."

"I have not betrayed you," Persephone says, looking up at me through her lashes.

"Then, prove it," I say, leaning in to whisper against her ear. "Prove you still have love for me. Prove that there may still be a chance for us, despite the many ways we have wronged each other."

"How?"

I pull back to give her a soft kiss on the lips before rising to help her to her feet.

"By telling me everything you learned today. Then, perhaps, I will find it in my heart to forgive you."

20

EROS

The moment I know Death and the mortal girl should be nearly back to my bedroom, I order everyone else to leave.

A ripple of laughter rolls through the crowd at this, setting my blood to boil.

"Out, get out before I have the lot of you writhing in pain instead of pleasure," I roar, rising to my feet in rage when they do not immediately obey.

As soon as they realize I am not joking, the space falls silent as my guests hurry to obey. I pace the empty gardens, my thoughts crashing and spinning about uselessly in my head.

Tonight, I find no joy in their presence, no satisfaction from their pleasure.

Instead, I only find disgust and self-loathing.

Not when I need to think.

Not when my mind is so fully consumed with *her*.

And for that, I require peace and quiet.

Death had asked for my plan. I let out a snort.

Plan? I have no plan. I was a fool to think I ever had one.

It is starting to make sense now why Death has such a hunger for the girl. Why he burns so bright in his possessiveness of her ... why he has an overwhelmingly endless desire to make her his.

And his alone.

She is everything that he is not.

Everything that we are not but wish to be.

She is life. Innocence. Hope ...

Light.

And yet, I feel like this is just beginning. There is something about her that makes her shine brighter than all the rest, and I still do not know what that is.

The more I get to know about her, the more her pull on me makes sense. The more it explains why I must suffer the same frustrating longing Death feels for her.

And after tonight, it further explains why I am so intoxicated by her mere presence. She is my opposite, as much as she is Death's, though in a different sort of way.

One touch, a single taste of her, and she sates me in ways that no other fallen creature has or could ever hope to. For one moment, I am saved from a lifetime of hunger and emptiness.

The craving she has aroused in me is unlike any I have experienced before. It is ravenous and all-consuming in its want.

But I know that I cannot simply take what I want from her.

I crave her, and yet, I am unable to conquer her in the same way I can the others.

No.

This power, she must be the one to come to me, to end my suffering as she feeds my hunger.

Only then will this longing dissipate, and I can be left to continue on as I was before she entered my life.

I must find a way to make her fall for me, to give in to me of her own desire.

But I do not know how with Death shadowing her every move. It already seems hopeless.

I continue to pace the garden, trying and failing to think of ways to deal with Death. If I could just find a way to get him to step aside, it would be so much simpler to get her to fall for me.

As it is, he is like an anchor, keeping her tethered to him even as he refuses to fulfill his own longing.

I pause suddenly in the middle of the garden as it finally hits me.

Death is her key, of course!

I do not need to get rid of him.

No, I just need to use him. Use his inaction, his inability to satiate his desire for her, to draw her closer to me. To drive her mad with a want that only I can then fulfill.

I will have to have more patience for this conquest than ever before, but I am certain, before too long, the mortal will seek me.

A grin pulls at the corner of my mouth at the thought.

It is almost too perfect.

Turning on my heel, I stride from the garden only to stop short as I reach the main hall. Pausing, I close my eyes, feeling for the presence that lurks just off to my right.

"Ah, Persephone," I say after a moment, "to what do I owe the pleasure of your company ... and at this time of night?"

"I have news," she says, her voice tinged with unease.

"Which is?"

"You have three days before Cerberus' return, but I can only keep him lost for so long. Hades is already suspicious of me."

"Three days? What am I supposed to do with so little time?"

"There was never any time to begin with," Persephone whispers sharply. "You know that as well as I do. Just ... try to find a way. For all our sakes. We need him on our side."

I sigh and give her a nod. I do not know how this is going to work, and I did not dare tell her what effect the mortal has had on me.

We are already tempting fate as it is.

She turns, and I listen to her footsteps retreat before making my way through the quiet halls of the palace toward my bedroom.

I know it would be too much to hope that Death is already asleep. I am sure he is waiting, watching, for my return, but I welcome that now.

His presence no longer feels like a thorn in my side now that I know how I will use it to get closer to her.

Reaching the end of the hall, I pause outside the doors. Pressing a hand to them, I close my eyes and allow myself to focus on the energies within the room beyond.

A shiver runs up my arm as I instantly get a wave of Death's presence ... I frown, my mind searching for the emotion but coming up blank. There is desire there, yes, but so much more.

There is a depth to the feeling that feels familiar, but I cannot quite pinpoint it.

Searching the room further, I feel the warm softness of the mortal's sleeping soul and am disappointed to find her still unreadable.

My thirst to know her, to learn what truly makes her so irresistible to me, grows worse with each passing hour. Realizing I will not learn any more about her like this, I open my eyes and push through the doors.

Instantly, Death shifts to look my way from a chair pulled next to the bed.

The fool.

If I were him, she would not be lying in bed alone but wrapped in my arms. Preferably after we had found our pleasure in each other. But, of course, that kind of behavior is far too *indecent* to expect of Death.

He is far too stubborn, bent on following his own self-imposed rules of morality, to allow himself to do something as unforgivable as *that*. Little does he know that by trying to do everything right by her, if he does not act on at least some of his feelings, he will only end up losing her.

But I welcome this oh-so-honorable fault of his.

I will teach the mortal what she needs to know, and I will win her from him in the end because of it. He will lose simply because I know *who* he is.

Signaling to the succubae I had ordered to attend and

watch over them, they excuse themselves, closing the doors behind them.

Without a word to Death, I begin to undress as I walk toward the bed. I can feel his cold glare fixed on me as I pull my shirt up over my head and toss it aside. It is only when I start to remove my pants that Death finally rises from his chair.

"What the hell do you think you are doing?" Death hisses.

"I am going to bed," I answer simply. "You may wish to stay up all night, but I do not."

"You will not sleep with her."

"Of course I will" I answer. "Though tonight, I only intend to sleep in *my* bed. This is my palace, remember? Even you lack the power to prevent me from joining her in it."

"Eros," Death lets out a low growl at this, the room growing even darker around him.

"Would you wake the mortal to test me? I do not have to give back your powers each time I take them, Death."

"I would give up everything if only it meant she was safe."

"I do not doubt it," I say, "but then, who will save her?"

His patience is wearing thin; I can feel it in the way his body tenses as he stares me down. He is not used to being challenged, let alone having to bend to his will to others. And yet, he would do it for the mortal in a heartbeat.

Curious.

What did she do to win such favor from a being as

powerful as Death?

Honestly, I thought it would be harder to get under his skin, but this is proving to be far easier than I was expecting.

"If you cannot stand the idea of me sleeping alone with her, then I suggest you join us," I say, reaching for the sheets. "I dare say some proper rest would do you good."

"No. She gets the bed, and we will make do elsewhere. It is not right."

"Speak for yourself," I snort, the atmosphere softly filling with the calming presence of flowers, thanks to Persephone's use of her own magic on me earlier. "I do not hold myself to the same standards. I am going to sleep in my own bed, regardless of what you decide. I will not sacrifice my comfort for the sake of your own moral quandaries. So, you can either watch me sleep with her or join us. It is as simple as that."

Though my use of Persephone's power is not nearly as strong, it is enough to keep him from stopping me as I slip into bed next to the girl. Still, as I turn on my side, my back facing them both, I can practically hear the crack of his clenched teeth as he decides what to do next.

It takes all of what little self-control I have not to shoot him a look over my shoulder to help sway his decision.

After a breath, the bed dips, and I hear him let out a deep sigh. I am almost impressed by my own work. I was starting to think he did not have it in him to join us in bed.

Perhaps my plan just might work after all.

21

DEATH

I am woken by a soft gasp, my body instantly freezing as the sound turns into a stifled moan of pleasure. Intense heat burns into me, filling my lungs with the heavy scent of indulged passion.

Hesitantly, I turn my head to find Hazel wrapped in Eros' arms, one of his hands held over her mouth as the other teases her breast.

My heart stops as rage bleeds through me, but before I can act, Eros' pale eyes lift to meet mine, and suddenly I find myself paralyzed. He gives me a devilish grin, teeth flashing as I struggle against the binds of his gaze, but to no avail.

I watch helplessly as he thrusts into her from behind, his other hand tracing over her curves before dipping between her legs. Her whimpers of pleasure break against his palm, shattering me to my core.

Eros' eyes remain locked on mine, forcing me to watch as he brings her to the edge of pleasure before joining her over it.

My heart races back to life as Eros' gaze releases me, and I hear him whisper his love to her before dropping his lips to hers.

Seeing black, I can't stop the wave of hatred and jealousy that crashes through me at this. My body returns to life, and I launch myself at him, only to suddenly find myself alone as I stare at a dark ceiling.

Frowning, I glance around me to realize I am back home in my own bed.

Hazel.

I turn my head to find her lying next to me, but as I lift myself up to look at her, I watch in horror as she slowly turns to bone before my very eyes.

My heart lurches as I reach for her but only come away with handfuls of dust as she slips through my fingers.

I let out a roar of anguish as I realize, yet again, that I have lost her.

I start, my breaths coming heavy and strained through my mask. Glancing beside me, I find Hazel still fully clothed in the silk nightgown she had been given by one of the succubae when we returned earlier.

Her breathing is soft as she sleeps peacefully in the middle of the bed, and it takes me a moment to realize what I saw was nothing more than a nightmare.

Though here, even a nightmare should not be disregarded too quickly. I glance over at Eros, who appears to be sleeping soundly, but try as I might, I am still unable to put my mind at ease.

Unable to resist the urge to protect her from my nightmares, I reach out and pull Hazel against my side, the heat of her burning into me as my heart finally settles. Pushing my mask up slightly, I take a deep, calming breath and fall asleep once more.

This time, with Hazel tucked safely by my side.

22

HAZEL

My eyes flutter open to utter darkness, a shiver racking my body as I find myself tucked against something hard and cold. I tremble again as another icy chill washes over me, blinking the sleep from my eyes as I try to make out the dark shapes around me without success.

I suddenly realize that I must have kicked off the blankets in my sleep. Blindly, I reach out a hand in search of them.

Instead, sparks of warmth shoot through my arm as my fingers find a wall of heat on the opposite side of me. I can't tell what it is in the dark, but my mind pushes this care aside as I wiggle closer to it. Pressing my back up against it, heat mixes with the numb chill that's crept into my body to leave me perfectly content in the ensuing warmth.

With a small sigh of relief, I drift back to sleep.

Eventually, I open my eyes to a pale light filtering into

the room, only to realize I'm exhausted, sticky, and covered in sweat. The silk nightgown that had felt so luxurious when I slipped into bed now clings uncomfortably to my skin.

Frowning, I try to remember what I dreamt, but try as I might, I can't quite seem to grasp any of the dreams that plagued my sleep.

A low half-growl draws my attention, and I am surprised to find Death sleeping next to me, his mask pulled up slightly to reveal his mouth and nose. His chest rises and falls softly as he sleeps. My heart skips a beat in my chest at the sight, a soft smile on my lips for a minute before it slowly fades in horror.

If Death is sleeping next to me, then whose arm is wrapped around my body?

Panic floods my body as I glance back to realize it's Eros I'm nestled against. His arm is snaked around me, holding me tightly to the heat of his chest as soft breaths ruffle strands of my hair.

Carefully, I reach to pry his arm from me, but his grip is firm and unrelenting as he continues to sleep. The weight of his arm is impossible as I struggle against him, only to have him shift in his sleep and pull me flush against his body ... and it's only now that I become fully aware of his desire for me.

My skin grows slick with sweat wherever his touches me, and I feel my body igniting involuntarily from within as the strength continues to drain from me with each passing second.

My eyes dart back to Death, my breaths coming

quicker with panic. He's sleeping deeply, unaware of my growing panic or my struggle to escape Eros' arms. Surely, if I could wake him, he would be able to help.

I reach out for him, straining to get to him, but he's just out of arm's reach.

"Death," I whisper weakly, my voice edged in fear.

Immediately he reaches up to pull down his mask, his eyes snapping open to meet mine. He sits up, his gaze darkening as he takes in my current situation. Without a word to me, he leans over and shoves Eros roughly aside.

Letting out a groan of pain, Eros' hold on me loosens as Death shoves him once again. Using his other hand to pull me free, Death cradles me against his chest as Eros rolls over onto his other side.

"Are you alright, little one?" he asks, worry in his voice.

I nod, welcoming the chill of his body against the sweat of my own.

"He ... he did not do anything to you?"

"No," I answer with a shake of my head.

"Are you sure?"

I lean away slightly to look up at him, confused why he keeps asking. Other than his hold on me, I'm sure he didn't do anything or touch any other part of me.

Still, I can't deny how troubled I am that I was completely unaware of him being in bed with me ... or that it was him, and not Death, I was cuddled up against. My cheeks burn with shame and embarrassment.

"Yes, I'm sure he meant nothing by it," I say, fighting the urge to bury my face against Death's chest.

He says nothing to this, but I can tell he doesn't quite believe Eros' innocence in all this. Tightening his hold on me, Death shifts forward to suddenly give him a hard shove from the bed.

Eros tumbles out, hitting the floor with a thud and a curse.

He groans loudly before rising to his feet with a glare that could almost rival Death's.

"That was *completely* unnecessary," he mutters as he stretches and rolls his shoulders.

My eyes widen as I realize he's not wearing anything. Standing before me, completely on display, is the man who just had me pinned to his chest.

I know I should pull my eyes away from the chiseled contours of his body as they trace their way lower, but I can't seem to stop staring. He looks like a marble statue, standing there in the soft morning light, but somehow even more beautiful.

And ... I gasp, heat rushing to my cheeks as my gaze drops too low.

Death coughs, the sound enough to break the draw Eros' body seems to have and pull me back to myself. With a small squeak of shame, I bury my face in Death's chest.

"Put some damn clothes on," Death growls.

Eros snorts but then sighs, and I peek out to watch him bend to reach for the sheet, wrapping it around his lower half. Then his eyes suddenly lift to meet mine, making my stomach twist as if he's looked straight into me. It unnerves me that, despite him appearing blind, he always seems to know where to find me.

He gives me a half-grin as if he's fully aware of the effect he's had on me, even if it was only momentary.

"The mortal does not seem to mind," Eros says. "Perhaps it is you cannot handle a little competition. In fact, judging from her reaction, perhaps she will even come to brave a taste before too long. I am sure I have plenty to offer her in the ways of pleasure."

Death tenses at this, his arms tightening slightly around me, but he doesn't respond. Choosing, instead, to starve Eros' ego by remaining silent. His focus returns to me as he searches my face, a softness to his eyes now that he's no longer glaring at a naked god.

"Are you sure that you are all right?" he asks, his voice gentle but edged with something sharp. "I would be *happy* to put Eros in his place if needed."

"I am," I say, shivering against the chill of his body. "I was just a little embarrassed, but I am fine otherwise. Truly."

"Very well."

I doubt Death would appreciate me going into details about my feelings anyway. Eros is the first man I've seen completely naked, and try as I might, the shock of it has burned an image in my mind. That and the surprise of finding two men in bed with me.

In truth, I would much rather just forget the last few minutes in their entirety. Well, *almost* in their entirety. I can't deny how my heart had leapt at waking to find Death so close, especially when he has always done his best to maintain certain boundaries between us.

"So, what are my lessons for the day?" I ask. "When do we start?"

"Start?" Eros says with a laugh. "We have already begun, have we not?"

I glance up at Death in confusion before turning to watch as Eros strolls leisurely across the room. It's a relief to have him gone from the edge of the bed, and I finally feel at ease to let my gaze wander around the room as he disappears into his closet.

"What do you mean by that?" Death asks, obviously frustrated when Eros doesn't offer further explanation.

Eros snorts, his soft chuckle preceding him as he steps out of the closet, now dressed in flowing white pants and a loose white shirt that hangs open down the center of his chest. I wait, more than a little impatiently, for him to answer.

"Is it not obvious?" he finally says when he glances our way.

Death lets out a low hum of irritation, but Eros' still doesn't relent. If anything, his grin widens as he walks back toward the bed.

"Out with it, Eros," Death says, his shadows curling up in frustration.

"Look," the pale god says, gesturing toward us, "in a matter of hours—and while I was sleeping, nonetheless, I might add—I have already managed to drive you straight into one another's arms. Now, just imagine what I could do with a few days' time."

His reminds me that I'm still nestled against Death's chest, his arms wrapped protectively around me as I all but cling to him. Frost seeps from his body into mine, but I savor the chill of him being so close.

I blush, wishing Eros hadn't drawn attention to it, as I

gently pull away from Death. He allows me to slip out of his arms, and I get out of bed as he sets about readjusting his clothes.

I cross my arms over my chest as the silk clings to me, hating the way it feels as though we've just been caught doing something shameful. Eros seems to agree, clicking his tongue in disapproval of our reaction.

"There will be no more of that," he says. "If you want my help, you are to respect the ways of my court from now on. Is that understood?"

"Which ones?" I ask before Death can refuse.

Eros' grin returns at my question.

"First and foremost," he says, "the manipulation of desire. You must learn to lean into it, to harness it, to use it in your favor. You must find ways to satiate it before it goes unchecked for too long."

"Why?"

"Simple, my dear mortal," Eros says. "Desire smolders, it can be contained with care, but once it gives over to lust ... Lust is a raging fire with a will of its own. A will that even I cannot control if the temptation grows too strong."

"I don't understand."

"Desire is an art. A dance of give and take. Give too much or too little, and all that remains is carnal need."

There's a warning in his voice as he glances between us, and I force myself to meet his gaze, reminding myself that he can't actually see me. His eyes just have an uncanny ability to pierce straight into the depths of my being. That's all.

"And given your current situation," he continues, his

smile slipping into something more serious, "that may prove to be a deadly game, indeed."

23

DEATH

My eyes narrow on Eros as I try to wrap my head around this so-called plan of his. If I am not mistaken, he means to teach Hazel to seduce Cerberus using me ... but this seems impractical.

Impossible even.

It is clear to me now that Eros can feel my desire for Hazel, whereas Cerberus must be won over completely.

These tasks are not one and the same, and I get the sense that there is more to this half-cocked plan of his than he is letting on.

I do not trust him, and I still have a hard time believing that he actually means to help us. He still has not told us exactly how this plan of his is supposed to work, and I am beginning to suspect he does not know.

Either way, I have no intention of letting him get anything past me. Hazel's safety and well-being are, and always will be, my first priority. Whether that means I must protect her from beasts, men, or gods, I will.

Even if it means I must protect her from myself.

"We must set some other rules, too," Eros says, pulling my attention back to where he now lounges in an armchair, his eyes fixed on Hazel.

"What rules?" I ask.

"You will do as I say, when I say it, and how I say it."

"Do not test my patience, Eros," I growl.

"Given the circumstances, I think it is *you* who should not test me," Eros replies, cocking his head to one side. "Now, we will begin with clothes. You are to wear what I give you without question. Last night was a good start, but—"

"Why do our clothes matter?" Hazel asks.

"*Your* clothes matter because you need to play a part that you do not yet have the confidence for. The garden was practically drowning in your mortification last night, which will not do. Cerberus will sense reluctance the moment he smells it. You must recognize your own power, learn to wield your feminine allure like the weapon it is."

"What does that mean?" I ask, despising the way he seems to say everything and nothing at all.

"It *means* we only have one shot at seducing Cerberus, and she must make him believe she wants him, in dress and behavior alike. Whether you like it or not, Cerberus has his weaknesses, just like every other man."

I remain silent as I watch him, trying to keep my thoughts to myself while I attempt to figure out what game he is playing at. Hazel's allure is not the kind that can be easily changed by mere clothing, and I worry that this is just another one of his ploys to get her in bed.

As far as I am concerned, she could wear a burlap sack, and still, it would not detract from her beauty or charm. She could wear nothing at all ... I blink, cutting this thought off as soon it comes to mind.

Regardless of what Eros might think, I do not see how Hazel's presence requires any changing at all.

Still, I hold my tongue for now.

"As for lessons, we ..." Eros pauses as I cut him off with a hard look. Sighing, he corrects himself, "*She* will be trained in the various arts of feminine seduction. At least, as much as possible, before Cerberus returns."

"Have you received word?" I ask.

"Yes, we have three days before he's expected back. I will prepare a test for her on the third day—"

"Three days," Hazel says softly, "is that enough time?"

"It will have to be if what Persephone told me is true," Eros answers.

"When did you have time to meet with her?" I ask.

"Last night, before I came to bed. She seems to have found a way to stall him, but even Persephone cannot be certain of how much time we have."

Hazel gives me a worried look at this before her brow furrows in thought.

"If Cerberus isn't guarding the gate, then can't we just slip through once Hades unlocks it?" Hazel asks.

"In theory, yes," Eros answers. "But, no."

"What Eros means to say," I explain, "is that Hades will not unlock the gate if Cerberus is missing. Guarded or not matters little, as long as it remains locked."

"Exactly, which is why we must continue on with my plans. The mortal will learn my arts so that by the time she encounters Cerberus, he can be brought to heel."

"What about the other souls?" Hazel asks. "The ones who arrive while Cerberus is away, surely they cannot be expected to roam the banks of the Styx."

"Yes," Eros answers, "and I suspect the river will claim its fair share of them."

Hazel blinks at him in horror before turning to look at me.

"But if you're here, then how is anyone dying?"

Her question makes me uncomfortable. It reveals just how much there still is that she does not understand about this realm, let alone the very nature of my being.

"My shadows," I answer, lifting one hand as I let some of the inky darkness swirl around it. "What you see around me is only a small portion of them; the rest fill the realms as an extension of myself."

Hazel tilts her head as she takes them in. I can already see the question that's forming behind her curious eyes.

"I only collect souls that require a little extra ... coaxing myself," I say. "Do not worry, little one, the shadows will not claim anyone whom I would not mark for death myself."

At this, Eros clears his throat. It would seem the attention has slipped away from him for too long.

Sighing, I turn my gaze back to him, and he grins as Hazel does the same.

"So, as I was saying, we have three days until the mortal's first test. In the meantime, I suggest you do exactly as I say, regardless of how unusual it may seem."

I let out a small sigh of displeasure at this, not liking

the smirk that settles over his face. I am sure there is more to this plan of his than meets the eye, but I will have to be patient to find out what it is.

Before whatever he is planning gets out of hand.

But, for now, I must bide my time. Even if that means allowing him to think he can tell me what to do.

Whatever this deal is that Hades made with the Fates … it must be truly terrible for them to allow a god like Eros more power. He hardly knew how to control what little he already had.

"Okay," Hazel says, answering for me. "I am sure we will both try our best and are grateful for your help."

I glance at her, happy to find she is watching me and not Eros. There is a soft, encouraging smile on her lips that gives me hope. She moves to lay a reassuring hand on my arm, and I look back at Eros.

"Very well, we agree to your terms for the time being."

"Finally," he says before striding back across the room to pull open the main doors. Waiting in the hallway are the two succubae from the day before. "Quickly, now."

They step in, their arms full of colorful garments and he motions for them to follow him into his closet. After a few moments, he returns with two outfits draped over his arms.

He gives me a look before shoving black pants and a shirt in my direction.

"I'm afraid this is all I have left in the way of black clothing," he says before turning to Hazel. "Not that I would ever dream of dressing *you* in anything so solemn. You, my dear mortal, need to shine brightly. Now, change."

Hazel glances at me before accepting the clothing from Eros and disappearing into the bathroom with one of the succubae.

"I think I will wear my own clothes today," I say, looking at the handful of fabric he has given me in disgust.

"I already sent them off to be cleaned."

"What?" I hiss, my eyes snapping to him.

"Do not worry. Your things are safe. Though, I was surprised by the boo—"

"Where is it?" I growl, my patience drawing thin as the room darkens around me.

"On the chair behind the screen," he answers quickly.

Glaring at him, I move behind the screen he points to near the bathroom. I let out a small sigh of relief at finding the book, as well as my other things exactly where he said.

Bending to pick them up, movement out of the corner of my eye draws my attention. Turning, I realize the bathroom door has not been closed all the way, leaving a small crack for me to see through.

Her back to me, I am momentarily entranced by the length of her bare leg, the soft curve of her hip ... and then I quickly look away as I realize that she is not wearing anything at all.

Shame sickens me as I chide myself for not looking away the moment that I realized the door was not fully closed.

I distract myself by focusing instead on putting on the new outfit that Eros has picked out. Stripping out of my clothes from the previous night, I shake out the shadowsilk and set it aside to give it a moment to breathe while I inspect my new garments. Holding up the new pair of pants, I suddenly realize there is absolutely no way these are going to fit.

Turning to grab the clothes I just took off, I suddenly find them missing.

"Eros," I growl, clutching the new pants over me for modesty. "Where the hell are my clothes? These new ones do not fit."

"Is that so?" Eros asks, drawing my attention as he steps behind the screen, his head cocking to one side as if sizing up my form. "Ah, I see. Just give me a minute to sort things out."

He disappears before I can say anything, and I abruptly find myself standing face to face with Hazel as she appears in the doorway just behind where Eros last stood.

"Hazel," I breathe, my heart thudding in my chest at the sight of her. I nearly forget my own indecency in the wake of her presence as I step slightly to one side to conceal the small book behind me.

"I-I'm so sorry," she gasps, her skin flushes, and I suddenly realize how little she is wearing. If I thought last night's dress was revealing, it is nothing in comparison to this one.

Eros seems to have forgotten to add fabric to the dress he gave her. The sheer dress falls to her feet in soft waves, but it does little to hide her body. Just enough of the white fabric has been layered across her breasts and hips to give it the illusion of modesty.

My body reacts against my hand, and I suddenly

worry that she will soon become aware of far more than just my naked torso.

"Eros, what is the meaning of this," I roar, twisting my shadows up around me to better conceal myself. "Explain yourself!"

24

HAZEL

I drop my eyes to the floor, my heart pounding so hard in my ears that I can barely think.

If I thought it was bad seeing Eros naked, seeing Death like this is so much worse. The moment I realized the state of his undress, my body practically burst into flames, nearly crippling me with unabashed desire for him.

Eros warned us of denying these feelings, but how am I supposed to appease them with a man I cannot touch?

"Apologies," Eros says, bursting back into the bedroom with a handful of dark fabric. "I nearly did not catch her in time."

He tosses the clothing to Death, who catches it in his free hand, before his eyes flash to me.

"Do you mind, little one?"

The heat burns more fiercely in my cheeks as I quickly turn away, realizing I'd started staring at him again.

Eros sits on the bed, smirking as we both wait for Death to finish dressing.

When he finally steps out from behind the screen, his hands are balled into fists at his sides. Shadows rise up to lick at him like inky flames as he points one gloved finger at Eros.

"Explain yourself."

"What is there to explain?" Eros says with a grin. "It was an honest mistake."

"Not about my clothes, about *hers*."

"Do you not like what you see?"

Death seems taken aback by this question, his eyes flickering to me before returning to Eros.

"Of course I do," he says, my heart skipping a beat in my chest, "but that does not matter."

"Why not?"

"She is *barely* covered, Eros. It is far too dangerous of a dress for her in a place like this."

"I thought you said you could protect her."

Death's eyes narrow on Eros, his shadows crashing around him, and I realize how close he is to breaking.

"Please, enough of this," I say, interrupting their fight as I hurry to put myself between them. "We agreed to his terms, and I am already wearing the dress."

"Very well," Death finally says with a sigh. "As long as you are comfortable with it."

"Of course I'm not," I say with a humorless laugh. "I've never felt more exposed in my life, but we are here for a reason. If Eros thinks this will help, I am willing to endure a few days of discomfort for a lifetime of possibility."

"You are right; forgive me."

I give him a comforting smile and nod before turning to look at Eros.

"What now?"

"Now, we go for a walk."

Rising, he crosses the room to offer his arm out to me. I glance at Death before tentatively accepting it, taking special care to make sure our skin does not touch.

Instantly, Eros tucks my arm against his side, pulling me closer to him than I would have liked. I'm not given a chance to argue or pull away, however, before he's already leading me from the room.

We make our way through the grand hallways of his palace, Death following warily behind me. As we walk, we encounter several of Eros' guests. Each time, Eros makes careful remarks on my behavior and posture, instructing me how to not only draw their attention but command it with a single look.

I try my best to listen, but I find his advice hard to apply when all I can focus on is their wandering eyes. Shame and frustration build in me as I realize just how far out of my own element I am.

Behind us, I can feel Death's disapproval wafting from him, and I wonder if I was wrong to accept this god's help.

Thankfully, Eros must realize that we're not getting anywhere because he suddenly turns and leads me toward the doors at one end of the hall. Opening them, we step out of the palace and into a lush garden.

My steps falter for a moment as I blink against the bright light to take in the sight before me. Greenery and flowers hang all around us, creating a covered pathway, a soft breeze rippling through them as we pass.

I take my time soaking it all in and find myself wishing for my paints and brushes to capture its beauty.

"This is a private garden," Eros says. "No one will bother us here. Perhaps I was too quick to expose you to the unknown. Let us start with something a bit easier."

Immediately, I feel my shoulders begin to relax as I let him pull me once more back to his side, the heat of him nearly overwhelming as we step out into the strange glow of the Underworld.

Tilting my head back, I let it wash over me. Closing my eyes, I can't help but think back to my time spent in the meadow with Death and Knax, and what I wouldn't give to be back there.

"Are you ready for your next lesson?" Eros asks, drawing my attention back to him as I open my eyes again.

I feel nowhere near ready for any of his lessons, but, of course, I don't say as much.

"Yes."

"Good, this way."

He pulls me through a heavy curtain of vines to one side, revealing a bright patch of soft grass where a picnic has been laid out on a yellow blanket. My eyes dance over the food spread out on it as my stomach lets out a growl that colors my cheeks.

"How is this a lesson—" I start.

"You are to ignore Death," Eros whispers in my ear, leading me toward the blanket. "Lie down, and place your head on my lap."

"I don't—"

"Hush, mortal, and do as you have been told."

I frown at him, but his tone reminds me that the time for questions has passed. Eros settles on the blanket, and I reluctantly do as I've been told just as Death pushes through the vines and into the clearing.

I can feel his gaze harden on us, and I have to fight the urge to remove myself from Eros' and run to him. To assure him that this is nothing more than a means to an end.

Even as I think this, I wonder what kind of end this is truly leading to.

"Join us," Eros says, plucking a grape and placing it between my lips before absentmindedly tracing the line of my jaw with his fingertip. I shudder at his touch, but I force myself not to move. "Tell me, Death, how does it feel?"

"How does what feel, Eros?" Death asks coldly, still standing in the clearing.

"To watch me touch her when you do not know her touch yourself? Eros asks, running a tender hand over my cheek before glancing up at Death.

Death bristles at his question, and I can see the fight gathering in his eyes. If Eros intends to continue pushing his buttons, I fear we will never make any progress. Unable to stop myself, I sit up and glare at the god.

"Death knows my touch, and I don't see how that is relevant to what you're supposed to be teaching me."

A strange look passes over Eros' face at my words. For just a moment, as his gaze moves over me, I swear he can truly see me despite his supposed blindness.

"How?" Eros asks, and I feel a blush creeping into my cheeks at his question.

"I had to end up here somehow, didn't I?" I answer quietly, my eyes dropping to my hands as they worry the sheer fabric of my dress.

"So, it was a lie then, when you told me you'd never taken anyone to bed?" Eros says, his eyes narrowing on me.

"No. I mean, we shared a moment. Together. But it ... we... I ..." my words tumble together, but I can't seem to close my mouth, let alone make sense of what I'm trying to tell him. Thankfully, Death clears his throat, drawing Eros' attention away from me.

"I kissed her," he says. "That is all."

Eros watches him for a long moment before turning back to me, a slow smile spreading across his face.

"Death can touch you?"

"No, the kiss is what killed me."

Eros cocks his head for a moment as he continues to study me. Then he glances across to where Death stands, warily watching him.

"Have you touched her since coming here?"

"Of course not."

"Why? It would be the first thing I tried if I were you."

Death opens his mouth before pausing and closing it. I find myself glancing up at him, suddenly just as curious. If I am already dead, could his touch really bring me any further harm?

"Because even I do not know what would happen," Death finally admits. "I cannot risk causing her even greater harm than I already have. I swore to protect her at all costs."

"Sometimes we must risk what we fear most in order to truly protect those we care about," Eros says, taking me by surprise. "At least, so my brother likes to often remind me."

"Even you should know how terrible that advice is when even Hades flinches at the thought of my touch."

"Yes, of course, but—"

"There is no but," Death cuts him off with a sharp look. "I will not test the limits of my power. Not on Hazel. Not when it means I could lose her forever."

25

HAZEL

Death falls quiet, and the rest of the picnic continues in awkward silence. Even Eros seems to be lost in thought; his only other order is to instruct me to eat my fill.

When I can finally eat no more, Eros rises and helps me to my feet.

"Let us try a different approach," he says, stepping away from me as Death eyes him warily. "Pretend I am Cerberus and try to seduce me."

I glance from him to Death, unsure how to proceed. "What should I do?"

"Whatever comes to mind," Eros says. "Let me see what I am truly working with. Approach me as if you want nothing more than to invite me into the warmth of your bed."

Death lets out a low rumble of disgust but otherwise remains silent.

Taking a deep breath, I steel myself for courage before lifting my head and stepping toward Eros.

"Wrong. Go back and try again."

I blink, taken aback by the abruptness of his correction. Feeling more than a little unsettled, I take several steps back and try again. I barely make it half a step before Eros is shaking his head and waving me back.

This happens several more times before I finally let out a cry of frustration.

"Are you going to teach me anything useful, or do you simply enjoy watching me humiliate myself?"

"Humiliate yourself," Eros says, the tone of his voice sending a chill racing down my spine as he pushes away from the tree. "No, I am breaking you."

"Breaking me?" I ask, Death tensing out of the corner of my eye as Eros steps closer.

"Yes, of everything you think will work on Cerberus. Stop thinking and just *be*. You will attract the same energy you feel within yourself. Win me over by first *wanting* to win me over. Make me feel it in every look, every word, every movement. Now, take a breath, and try again."

I close my eyes and allow myself a moment to reset. Slowly, I open them again to look up at Eros, and for a split second, I *feel* it. Feel the energy I'm meant to be harnessing.

"There it is, good mortal," Eros says with a purr of satisfaction.

No sooner than he says this, and I realize I'm trying to connect this feeling with Eros, the energy disappears, leaving me feeling flushed and more disheartened than ever.

"Again."

No matter how hard I try, I'm unable to replicate that split second of understanding again. Eros is unrelenting in his tutelage, but still, I find myself unable to draw on that energy again.

It's not working, and I can't help but look to Death as Eros' lessons only seem to become more and more useless to me. I'm starting to fear that he won't actually be able to teach me in time.

Even Eros' patience seems to be drawing thin as he runs a hand through his white hair. He turns in a small circle before facing me again, this time tearing off his shirt to toss it aside.

"Look at me," he says, gesturing toward himself. "Is this not enough to inspire you? How am I supposed to—"

"Eros, enough," Death says. "You cannot expect her to learn everything in a single afternoon."

"She has learned nothing!"

"Enough! Take us back to the room; we can continue discussing this once everyone has had a chance to calm down."

Eros' jaw hardens, but then, much to my relief, he nods.

"Fine."

I want nothing more than to thank Death for ending the lesson, though I know better than to do so in front of Eros. We're led back through the palace, Eros remaining strangely quiet the entire way.

Reaching the doors, he pushes them open and steps back.

"I have some business to attend to. I'll have dinner sent up."

With that, he turns and sweeps out of sight.

Neither Death nor I say anything as we slip into the room, shutting the door behind us. It's a welcome relief not to have Eros hovering.

"I cannot stand that man," Death says, turning toward me. I can feel his displeasure rolling off him in heavy waves. Even the darkness around him seems to have grown inkier with his mood. Thick shadows waft up around him, nearly swallowing his form within them. I'm not sure what to say as I stare up at him.

"He has his head so far up his own ass ... how the hell does he expect to teach you anything when it is obvious that he barely understands his own craft."

I'm so taken aback by his directness that I can't seem to find any words in the way of a response. Death shakes his head, letting out a sigh of frustration as he moves to step around me. Only, I mistake his path, and he nearly collides with me instead.

I reach out, my hand meeting the firm expanse of his chest as he quickly grabs my arms to keep from tumbling to the floor.

He goes still, slowly lowering his eyes to meet mine. "Forgive me, Hazel; I am not thinking clearly."

"Your frustration is understandable," I say softly. "I feel it as well, but we need his help. I just need time to grasp what he's trying to teach me."

I can tell he wants to argue with me, and for a moment, I think he will. But then Death lets out a deep sigh, the fight leaving his body as his shadows calm into soft waves at his feet.

"You are right. It is my own fault for feeling ..."

He trails off, and I wait a few seconds before pressing, "Feeling what?"

"Nothing."

"Please, I need to know what you're thinking. We're in this together, aren't we?"

He stares down at me, his eyes softening as they move over my face.

"I just ... I do not trust Eros. I think he is trying to seduce you more than he is actually trying to help."

I let out a sigh at this, pulling out of Death's hands as I walk further into the room. I don't know why I'd hoped for more from him, some vocal acknowledgement of his feelings for me.

"At least he's *trying* to help," I say, regretting the tone of my voice as soon as it slips from me.

"You think *that* was helping? He spent the entire day speaking nonsense and giving you useless pointers," Death growls.

"Well, you're wrong," I say, my back now to him, "because, for a moment when I was with him, I felt a connection."

"Fine."

Death strides past me at this, his shadows crashing over me in an icy wave as he crosses the room to settle into a chair.

"What should we do now?" I ask.

"Wait," he answers bluntly, not looking my way. "I am sure Eros will return to teach you more *lessons* before too long."

I try not to notice the distance he's put between us as I quietly move to sit on the bed. The minutes slip by slowly, the silence filling the room almost nauseating in its intensity.

Just when I'm about to open my mouth to try to break the tension between us, there's a knock.

Death rises immediately and strides across the room to throw open the doors. He almost seems disappointed when it isn't Eros but the two female attendants. One of which is carrying a covered tray.

"Your dinner," she says, stepping into the room to place it down on the bed beside me. "Afterward, we will help you prepare for bed."

"Eros will be late returning tonight," the other woman says, her gaze slipping to Death before returning to me.

I eat in silence as Death paces the room, and I start to worry that we won't have another moment alone to talk. After finishing my meal, one of the attendants leads me into the bathroom to bathe and dress me while the other sets to work starting a fire.

The nightgown she gives me is little more than a thin layer of silk, barely opaque enough to conceal me while still clinging to my form.

"Beautiful," she says, with an approving look. "Now, go to him."

"Oh, no," I say quickly, shaking my head.

"Why not?"

"I ... I can't."

She laughs at this before realizing I'm serious.

"But you must," she says.

"He doesn't want me in that way, trust me."

"Nonsense, go to him. Let him see you like this. Unless it is you who doesn't want him?"

I open my mouth to answer but suddenly realize I can't. Perhaps she's right. The woman gives me an encouraging look as she and the other servant gather their things and leave.

Death is sitting in an armchair by the large window, watching the city come to life in the growing darkness. Cautiously, I make my way over to him, my heart pounding in my chest.

"Sydian," I say softly, and he slowly turns to glance back at me.

His eyes widen as they take me in, the iciness of his shadows pouring around me, making my breasts take shape beneath the thin fabric.

"Hazel, I—" I don't know what comes over me as I suddenly reach for his mask. Death catches my wrist in his gloved hand just as my fingertips brush against it, a low growl rolling from him. "No."

"But—"

"I said no."

The firmness with which he says this has me shrinking back on myself. I knew I shouldn't have listened to that woman.

"I'm sorry," I whisper, my voice cracking. Shame burns my cheeks as I quickly step back.

"Hazel—"

Pulling my wrist from Death's grip, I turn and quickly make my way over to the bed, hoping to hide my shame beneath the covers.

I hear Death sigh from his corner of the room before rising and then the soft thud of his boots drawing nearer.

I quickly close my eyes just as the door suddenly flies open with a bang.

Sitting up, I watch as a very drunk Eros stumbles in, and Death changes course to put himself between us.

Eros makes a tutting sound as he waves a hand in our direction. Death tenses as though preparing for whatever verbal attack Eros is about to launch.

All I can do is glance between them as I clutch the blanket to me, hoping that the two aren't about to entangle themselves in another fight.

"Such a shame not to catch the two of you in bed together," Eros says, his words coming out slightly slurred as he leans against the doorway.

"How dare you imply such a thing," Death seethes. "I would never—"

"You would never?" Eros snorts, his grin widening as he turns his head toward Death. "Have you forgotten the rules already? Or do you truly wish to deny your feelings for the mortal?"

As he says this, there's suddenly such clarity and sharpness to Eros that I almost can't believe it. Was he faking being drunk just a moment before?

Not that it matters as my eyes slip to Death, my heart pounding in my chest as I wait for him to say something.

Death has gone unnervingly still; though his back is to me, I can imagine the narrow of his inky black eyes as they stare Eros down.

"What?" Death finally asks.

"Do you not lust for the girl, Death?"

There's a long pause, and I'm certain the two of them can

hear my heart as it beats wildly in my chest. No matter how hard I try to tamper down the hope that has sprung to life inside me, I'm unable to. I'm desperate to hear Death's answer, desperate to know that I am not alone in my feelings.

I lean forward on the bed as Death takes a deep breath.

"No, Eros. You are mistaken when it comes to my feelings for her."

26

HAZEL

My heart shatters into a thousand tiny little shards at this.

I knew, all along ... I knew it was too good to be true.

I've been idealizing every moment of tenderness I thought passed between us. Every gentle touch and longing gaze, every half-smile. His kindness had morphed into something more powerful, borne out of my desperate need to be loved.

How could I have been so foolish?

He is Death, after all. Deadly and all-powerful. Terrifying even in his beauty. Known by every living thing and feared by nearly all of them.

And then there's me.

Nothing more than a simple mortal. A mere human of little consequence ... and a dead one at that.

Deep down, I've always known this. Known that he could never feel anything for me.

Still, there had been hope.

Some small part of me had thought it possible. The part of me that had believed the fairytales I grew up with. That believed there was a happy ending out there for me. The part of me that had always thought maybe, just maybe, there was a chance that Death could love me the same way I do him.

Where Merelda and her sons had failed to break me, Death finally has.

Tears well in my eyes as I try to fight them back. I will not allow Death, or Eros, to see me cry. For either of them to piece together the true nature of my feelings for him.

It's bad enough that I know what a fool I've allowed myself to be. I don't want them privy to that knowledge as well ... but I fail as a small sob escapes me.

Immediately, both Eros and Death turn toward me.

In a breath, Death is kneeling before me beside the bed, his eyes soft as he searches my face worriedly.

He doesn't touch me as he tries to soothe me, and that nearly makes the tears come faster. I hate the confirmation that he's only here because he feels responsible ... guilty over the loss of my soul.

"Hazel," he says, his voice painfully soft. "What is it? What is wrong?"

I can't find my voice, my tears choking me as I try in vain to regain control of my emotions. It's a losing battle, though, as stifled sobs escape me despite my best efforts. Tears stream down over my cheeks.

Death raises a gloved hand, reaching to brush away them from my cheeks, but I flinch away from his touch. He pulls back, and I use the opportunity to turn away from him, clutching the sheets tighter around me.

Death rises but is careful to keep distance between us, as though he can sense the way my heart is shattering over and over again. He seems unsure of what to do as he glances at me.

Then his eyes land on Eros, who watches uncertainly from across the room.

"This is your fault," Death accuses him, taking a step toward him.

"Me," Eros scoffs in disbelief. "What did I do?"

"You are trying to get between us, to divide us with your vulgar rules and questions."

Eros tosses his head back to laugh at this, giving Death a chance to storm across the room. Eros' eyes go wide as Death grabs the front of his shirt, hauling him out of the doorway and slamming him up against the wall, and a small gasp of surprise escapes me as I watch.

"Why?" Eros says, holding onto Death's arm as he struggles to free himself. "Why would I do that? What reason do I have?"

"I see what you are doing, and I won't stand for it. Not for another moment."

"Again, give me one good reason," Eros hisses.

"You mean to claim her for yourself and keep her soul trapped here with you."

Silence meets Death's accusation. I glance between the two of them in shock, frowning as I see the way Eros won't meet our eyes.

Surely that can't be true. I mean, Eros had made it obvious he didn't mind taking certain liberties with me, but to actually desire me, let alone want to trap me here?

The way Eros' body stiffens as Death presses him harder into the wall has me questioning everything.

"Yes, I do." Eros admits, "I crave her with every fiber of my being. I want to make her mine, to know her touch, her body, her soul in every way. Can you honestly blame me for that? You may deny your feelings, but I will not. I am the God of Lust; after all, it is literally in my nature. But I was not trying to trap her here. I swear that on all the gods."

His words only fuel Death's temper as inky shadows begin to crash around him. The dark storm clouds from before returning as his grip tightens.

"I would end you here and now," Death snarls, raising his free hand to his mouth to yank off his black glove.

I stare in shock for a split second, hardly daring to believe he actually means to end Eros' life right before my eyes.

I can't allow him to do that. I leap out of bed, running across the room before he can bring his hand down on Eros.

"No!" I shout, wrapping my hands around Death's bicep.

It's a miracle that he stills his hand just inches from Eros' face as he turns to stare down at me, his eyes bottomless voids of fury behind his mask.

Tears still stain my cheeks as I carefully move around him, though I don't spare Eros a glance as I squeeze between the two men.

To my surprise, Death doesn't immediately back down this time, even as I put my hands against his chest.

"Please, spare him," I plead, my voice strained. "Please, Death. For me."

Just like that, he drops Eros and takes a step back from us. The shadows still swirl around him as he pulls himself up, towering over me as he shoots a glare at Eros. Then a softer look at me, one that's laced with pain and something I can't quite understand.

Without a word, he turns on his heel and storms from the room.

I watch the doors close behind him, unsure of what I should do now. Part of me wants to chase after him, but the other part of me wants to throw myself in bed and cry myself to sleep.

Except, I don't trust Eros enough to do that, especially after what he just said.

Turning back, my gaze narrows on him.

"I suppose I should—"

"Is there any truth to what Death said?" I interrupt.

"You will have to be a bit more specific than that, mortal."

"Are you trying to turn Death and me against one another?"

"I did not realize that was an optio—"

"Then it is also not true that you want me ... you simply wished to get a rise out of Death, right?"

He frowns.

"No, I was being honest about that. I cannot and will not deny my desire for you, but I seem hardly to blame for Death's reaction. How was I to know he would have such a visceral reaction to me asking about his feelings for you?"

"What do you mean?"

He hesitates, but I can see in the way his smile fades that he understands the meaning behind my question. I wait as he works out how to best to explain himself, not that I have much of an option.

Without Death, I am stuck here in this palace, if not this room.

"Because Death cares deeply for you," Eros finally says. "More than I have ever seen him care for anyone or anything."

"Then you aren't simply trying to hurt me to get at him?"

"Of course not. I do not wish you harm."

I narrow my eyes on him, hardly believing a word coming out of his mouth. If Death doesn't trust him, I doubt I should either. I'm not interested in being told pretty lies simply to have another man, however beautiful he may be, try to bed me.

His expression grows serious, as though debating whether or not to elaborate on what he's said. Eros steps toward me, reaching out a hand to gently tuck a strand of hair away from my face. He doesn't even seem to mind that I flinch away from him at his touch.

Catching my chin, he forces me to look up at him.

"I meant every word I said," Eros says, his voice low and velvety. "I will not harm you, but I will not pretend that I do not crave you in every way, and more than I have desired anyone before."

"How can you say that?" I ask. "You've barely known me a day."

"When you have lived as long as I have, a day is

more than enough to know exactly what you want when you see it." I can't help but snort at his casual use of the term, and he seems to sense the irony of it. "Despite what you may think, I can see, just not in the same way you can. In fact, I daresay I can see more than most."

The heat of his touch spreads through me, his voice melting over me in a way it hadn't since the first day we were here. There's no pretense to his tone, no arrogance, none of what I've come to know him as. There is only deep sincerity, yet I force myself not to give in, not to feed it. Perhaps this is just another one of his tricks.

Besides, I've obviously been wrong before; why should I trust what I'm feeling now?

"What do you mean by that?" I ask, drawing on what remaining courage I have as I search Eros' face.

He blinks, seemingly taken aback by my question. I don't let my gaze drop as I wait. It matters little how long it takes. There's no chance of me getting sleep until I've come to understand this mess I've ended up in the middle of.

"It means that I have seen the true beauty of your soul without ever having lain eyes on you. It means you have captured me unlike any other I have ever known. I would know your soul amidst a thousand others, forsaking them to get to you."

My frown deepens as I wait for some laugh or teasing smirk to pull at his lips. I get neither, as his expression and tone remain serious.

In a way, I suppose I shouldn't be surprised by a confession like this from him. After all, as he said earlier, he is the God of Lust. Of course, he would tell me sweet nothings.

He wants to bed me. That's his nature.

Perhaps I've been too harsh in my judgment of him. If Death truly has no feelings for me, why shouldn't I enjoy Eros' attention?

It may not be love, but that doesn't mean I couldn't find some pleasure in it. If nothing else, perhaps doing so would finally help give me some clarity. Perhaps it will be what I need to let go of Death and these fantasies I've allowed to consume my heart and mind.

To go back to the life that I knew before I ever met him.

27

EROS

I am startled by my own confession. It was as close to confessing love as I have ever come ... and yet, I still cannot determine what the mortal feels for me. What would my brother say if he knew?

The tension forming between us is almost unbearable; my own cravings intensified by her nearness to me.

But from her, I can sense nothing.

I watch as she pulls away from my touch to pace the room, lost in her own thoughts and feelings.

It is driving me mad, obviously, to have confessed my desires to her with no certainty that they are or ever will be returned. Even now, I can do nothing but stand here wondering.

One touch of her skin, and I would do anything to have her.

I would give up my palace. Forsake all other lovers. Forgo all that brings me pleasure just to have a taste of her.

To feel her energy at my fingertips. To know the satiation that I had felt after our kiss.

I can only begin to imagine what losing myself completely to her would feel like, and this need to know fuels me almost as much as my own desire for her.

But for now, I must be patient.

I will not take what she is unwilling to give.

I do not know why Death will not admit to his feelings for her unless I truly am mistaken.

No, impossible.

I have never felt anything more powerful than what I have felt from him for the mortal. Even as I think this, a pinch of jealousy twists my gut. It almost makes me laugh out loud.

Me, jealous?

I force the thought aside. *I* do not get jealous. Not for anything or anyone.

Still, I know this is a lie when I feel the way the girl's gaze continues to slip toward the closed doors as she paces.

Even now, she still waits for him. Hopes for his return.

"You should sleep," I say when her feet start to drag in exhaustion.

"Not until he comes back."

"You need your strength for the sake of your body and soul."

"What do you mean?"

"You are still connected by a thread to life, not having completely crossed to the other side."

"So?"

"The food and sleep you partake in here, they will help sustain your body to some extent. Delaying the effects of time, however little."

She pauses in her back and forth and lets out a sigh.

"Fine, but you must promise you will not come near me as long as Death has not returned."

"I swear it," I say, hating the words and the fact that I mean them the moment they leave my mouth. I move past her, settling on a lounge in the hopes of easing her mind.

She hesitates a moment longer before crawling into bed, pulling the covers up over her frame. As if she has already forgotten about me, her thoughts so preoccupied with Death.

I want nothing more than to join her, to slip beneath the sheets and show her pleasure unlike anything she has ever imagined. To hear my name on her lips as she unspools around me. To ruin every other man for her, showing her things no other would be able to give her.

Though, I suppose it would not be that difficult, seeing how no one has yet lain with her.

I clear my throat as it suddenly dawns on me how undeserving I am of her, and it terrifies me. She terrifies me.

For the first time in my life, I do not fully understand myself. Not when I am around her. The hunger I feel in her presence, the all-consuming hold she has on my body and mind.

I turn my head toward the girl, relishing the soft rise and fall of her chest as sleep takes her. I could spend an eternity sitting here, watching her sleep, and never once bore of it. Never want or desire for another's companionship.

Death's feelings suddenly make sense.

Could this be what my brother means when he speaks of love?

No.

I shake the thought from my head with a snort of incredulity.

Love is not for me; I am the God of Lust.

She is nothing more than another conquest. A challenge unlike any before her that I fully intend to see through.

I will win her to my bed, and then, I can return to my duties. To the pleasures of life that I knew before her.

Soon, she will be nothing more than a faint memory. A distant recollection of a time that a mortal came close to bringing the God of Lust to his knees, nothing more and nothing less.

The night begins to drag on, and still, Death does not return.

I find it harder and harder to remain in the chair as I had promised. With each passing minute the temptation to join the mortal in bed grows stronger. My desire to have her in my arms burns through me with ever-increasing intensity.

And yet, I can do nothing but wait.

This is by far the longest I have ever gone without giving in to my own desires. The longest I have ever had to. I am not one to deny myself pleasure, and I have never been denied ... but since the mortal's arrival, I have found that no one else will do.

No one else has been able to hold my attention since our kiss.

I have tried, nonetheless, but found myself unwilling or unable to perform with any but her. My cravings are slowly evolving into unrelenting hunger, and she the only one who can sustain me.

Finally, unable to bear the torment of my hunger any longer, I stand. Stretching, I turn to leave the room, not trusting myself to be alone with her as the hour grows too late and my desires burn their hottest. I will not allow myself to break my promise to her.

Opening the door, I step into the hall before coming to an abrupt stop as I take in the shadows lurking there. Letting out a frustrated sigh, I pull the door closed behind me.

It seems that Death was not far off this whole time.

"Where the hell have you been?" I hiss.

"I never left," he answers. "I promised to protect Hazel, no matter what the cost was to myself. She may have stayed my hand against you, but that does not mean she will not need my assistance again."

"You mean you were eavesdropping."

"No, I did not listen to your private conversation."

"Then how would you know if she needed your help?"

"Similar to you, I would have felt it," he says coldly, his shadows spilling out around me in an icy wave.

"Well, obviously, you need more practice," I bite back.

"Otherwise, you would have realized she was waiting for you to return for the better part of an hour."

My annoyance grows as I realize hours have passed since she went to bed. Hours that I could have been sleeping happily next to the mortal now wasted because this stubborn fool would rather stand out here than admit the truth of his feelings. Or, at the very least, give her some explanation.

"Come back into the room so we can finally get some rest."

"No, it is best I do not upset her any further."

"I am far too tired to waste more of my breath arguing with you," I say. "I would like to sleep in my bed, and if that means I must find a way to drag you into it, then so be it."

"Do not make me laugh," Death snorts. "I should have known you would stop at nothing to get what you want."

"And yet, I have."

"What?"

"Your mortal will not allow me near the bed without you. It seems that if I would like to sleep in my own bed, then I must share it with you."

Death's shadows pull back slightly at this.

"Is this true?"

"Yes, now, will you join us in bed so that I can finally get some sleep?" I ask, turning to push open the doors.

Death hesitates for a moment before moving past me, and I follow him back inside the room. If I could, I would have left him out in the hall, letting his mind wonder as to what was happening between us.

But I know that Hazel will never allow me to claim her, any part of her, without him. So, if that is the sacrifice that I must make to be close to her, then so be it.

I will suffer Death's presence to win her favor

28

HAZEL

I groan, waking to find myself covered in a damp sweat. Again, as I shift, I find that an arm is flung over my hips, anchoring me to a sleeping Eros.

I freeze as I peer around the room; it seems that he was unable to keep his promise to me. Death is nowhere to be found.

I should have known better than to trust him. Anger at myself and my naivety fills me as I attempt to wriggle my way out of Eros' arms.

Despite what he told me last night, I am still uncertain about him and his intentions ... and this just proves I shouldn't let my guard down around him.

Eros' arm feels heavier than ever, and no matter how much I squirm, I'm unable to free myself. My heart pounds in my chest as I worry that I'm just making things worse as I feel him shift behind me.

Movement draws my eyes to the corner of the room. I squint against the darkness as I try to make out what is there.

"Death?" I whisper.

Almost immediately, the darkness takes the shape of Death. He steps forward, coming to crouch before the bed. Our eyes meet, and I try to ignore the way my pounding heart calms at the sight of him.

He was here, after all. He didn't leave me alone with Eros.

"Yes, little one?" he asks, his voice strained but gentle, my heart aching in my chest at the sound of his voice.

"I need …" I want to know why he was lurking in the shadows across the room instead of lying next to me, but I bite my tongue to stop myself from asking. "I need your help. I can't move."

For a moment, I swear I see disappointment in his eyes as he watches me, but then he nods, standing and breaking our eye contact. Surely, I'm just seeing what I want to, what I *wish* was there. Sleep must still have some claim over me.

He says nothing as he leans over me, and I'm all too aware of how careful he is to keep space between us. He never once touches me as he lifts Eros' arm off of me, allowing me to slip away from his side.

"Thank you."

"Of course," Death says, slipping back into his shadows, as if being near me is the last thing he wants. My heart clenches at this thought, but I refuse to allow tears to fill my eyes.

It's better this way. It's better to know now to prepare myself for returning to my life before Death.

I curl up on the far side of the bed, closing my eyes as

I wait for dawn to finally break. All too slowly, the darkness fades, and I slip from bed.

The moment my feet touch the floor, Eros sits up. I watch as he rubs the sleep from his eyes before shooting a half-grin my way.

"Come back to bed," he says.

"No, thank you," I answer with a snort and shake of my head. "There is far too much for us to do to spend the day in bed."

Eros cocks his head to the side as he watches me, the slow smile that spreads across his face making me aware of my mistake.

"Am I not meant to be teaching you the ways of seduction?" he asks. "It seems to me that the bed is the perfect place to do just that. In fact, I think it is exactly where I would prefer to teach your next lesson."

My cheeks burn at his suggestion, and I quickly say, "There is still far too much for me to learn before I need skills that ... require a bed."

He grins at this as he sits up, stretching and revealing the bare expanse of his chest.

"Fine, what are a few more days of delayed gratification but added pleasure anyway?"

I let out a nervous laugh as I try to decipher just how serious his words might be, my stomach twisting nervously as I realize they're probably more serious than I think. Especially with the way his eyes seem to linger on me as he finishes his stretch.

Slipping from the bed, I realize that, once again, he isn't wearing anything. My entire body flushes as I glance away, wondering what Death must think to know I'd been in bed all night with a naked Eros.

As if reading my mind, I hear a growl of disapproval from the shadows, drawing my attention to them. Death still stands, cloaked in darkness as he watches us... well, watches Eros, his eyes narrowed as he glares at the God of Lust.

"Stare as much as you like," Eros laughs. "After all, is that not what I was made for? To bring pleasure to all those around me, even the likes of you. Besides, it is not as if I can see, so you might as well do it for me."

Unable to stop myself, I glance over at him as he gestures toward his pale eyes, his smile slipping for just a moment. Bitterness edges the corner of his mouth as he lets out a sigh, turning his back on us.

"Funny, is it not? The God of Lust and Desire being blind to all physical beauty, at least in the most literal of senses. Perhaps the Fates do have a sense of humor after all."

"Have you always been blind?" I ask, the question slipping out before I can bite my tongue.

I flinch at the way the room falls quiet. Eros stills as he continues to face away from me, but at least his shoulders don't tense at my question.

I didn't mean for my curiosity to get the better of me, and I hate to think that I have just offended him.

Turning to look over his shoulder at me, he hesitates for a moment before answering, "No. Not always, but it has been so long now that any memories of what I once saw have long since faded. I have learned to use my other senses to my advantage, though. With them, I am more than capable of painting an image, if you will, in my mind."

"It doesn't sound too dissimilar to painting on a canvas."

"In a way," Eros says thoughtfully. "Though, it is not always images that I see. Often it is a sense of emotion, wants, the true expression of a being. In fact, if you had not come here with Death, I might even suggest I know your soul better than most."

I glance over to where Death stands at the mention of him. He remains stoically quiet, almost seeming to pull further into himself as he watches Eros with wary eyes. His silence and the gentle curl of his shadows making him unreadable, even to me.

"Come," Eros says, pulling the sheet from the bed to wrap around his waist and lifting a hand to beckon me. "Let us find you a new dress."

After a moment's hesitation, fighting the urge to steal another glance toward Death, I move to follow Eros.

Eros leads me into his massive closet, bypassing more clothes than I've ever seen at once. He runs his hands over the clothing as he walks deeper into the room, occasionally pausing to tilt his head to the side before moving on.

"What are you doing?" I ask, watching him curiously.

"Finding you the right dress," he replies. "This one will not do. It will only illicit feelings of jealousy in the wearer, and this one ... is far too depressing. Hmm."

"You can feel the dresses ... intentions?"

He shrugs.

"In a sense. Though it has more to do with the

garment's feel in relation to its intended wearer. Take this one, for example," Eros says, pulling out a pale peach dress. "I do not have to see to know this one would make you fade into the background, draining you of energy. And this one, the cut is far too sharp, the color too angry. It would only draw the attention of those who wish harm upon you."

He tosses a bright pink dress to one side before holding up another, then another. He gives me an explanation each time as to why they're wrong for me.

I can't help but be curious as I step closer, fascinated by his ability to read the dresses. It seems to matter little to him what they actually look like but more what potential they hold.

"This one," he says, holding up a light blue dress. "This is the one."

It's pretty hanging from his fingers, as they all have been, but I can't help frowning at it. Even from several feet away, I can tell there's very little fabric to it. I'm growing tired of walking about, feeling as though I'm completely exposed to the world.

I prepare myself, nonetheless, for him to hand it over and order me to wear it.

Only he doesn't.

"You do not like it."

"It's not that," I say quickly. "It's beautiful, truly. It's just not me."

"Then look through the dresses here and find one that you would prefer to wear," he tells me.

This takes me by surprise, and I stare at him in disbelief for a moment before tentatively reaching out.

I run my fingers over the dresses, but nothing jumps out at me, and I don't get any of the senses that Eros mentioned. I only finally come to a stop when I discover an empty hanger.

Pushing aside the dresses around it, I realize that it's not empty. The dress was just hung incorrectly, causing it to slip off.

No wonder Eros walked right past it. It would've been impossible for him to know there was anything here just by running his fingers over the garments.

Pulling the dress out, I let out a gasp.

It is the most gorgeous white gown I have ever seen. It shimmers in the light like a thousand twinkling stars as I run my fingers over the delicate fabric.

It's on par with the ethereal beauty of the silky black gown Death gave me ... and it has far more fabric to it than most of the dresses here.

Combined.

I can feel Eros as he comes up behind me, reaching around me to touch the dress in my hands. He inhales sharply the moment his fingers brush against it.

In a heartbeat, he's backed up several steps. I turn to watch him, confused by the way he frowns down at me. It's obvious he knows exactly what dress I am holding by the way he narrows his gaze at it.

"Not that one."

I frown, my heart sinking.

"But—"

"No," he says, cutting me off. "You may choose another dress. Any dress. Just not that one."

Disappointment creates a pit in my stomach as I run

my hands over the gown. I already know it's the only one that I want.

Even though I know there's no point fighting him over this, I consider it for a moment. I don't want to wear any of the barely-there dresses that he seems to have selected for me. This is the dress that calls to me. I can practically hear it begging me to slip into it.

Sighing, I give the dress one last longing look before I carefully place it back on the hanger and put it back. I hesitate a moment longer, letting my fingers linger on it for a moment before I pull away.

Taking several steps along the rack, I try to return to choosing a dress, but none of the ones I see interest me. None of them call to me as that one did. Turning, I look back to where Eros stands, a strange look on his face.

"I can't choose one," I tell him.

He blinks as though remembering that I'm still here, and then he hands me the light blue dress in his hands.

I realize that I have no choice but to accept at this point.

Before I have a chance to ask him why he chose this dress, he turns and reaches for clothes of his own. I watch after him as Eros leaves me standing alone in his closet, confused.

I can't piece together what I did wrong as the female attendant from the day before suddenly appears. She quickly helps me into the dress before setting to work on my hair.

As expected, the light blue dress barely covers me. I sigh as I stare down at myself, running my hands over the gauzy material. As the woman makes several final touches, I make my way out of the closet and toward whatever Eros has planned for me.

I may not know the ways of this palace or understand what is expected of me, but I am starting to realize that I do not belong here. I have never belonged here or with Death, no matter how much I wish it weren't true.

The sooner that I can get away from this place and these beings, the better off I'll be.

29

HAZEL

Eros seems off as we go about starting our day. He's distant as we wander the halls of the palace, not once instructing me how to present myself or otherwise greet the others we pass, Death carefully remaining several paces behind us.

Even as we step into another one of the stunning gardens, this one fully blocked from outside view by high walls of blossoming vines and twisted trees, Eros remains quiet. His gaze doesn't so much as dip to me once, no matter how often I glance up at him.

Normally, I would welcome his silence, but something about his expression has me wishing he'd speak.

Until he starts ordering me about.

The change in his demeanor is so sudden it takes me completely off-guard.

Eros leans against a tree as he begins instructing me how to walk, talk, and simply exist in front of a man I'm trying to win over. He barely glances at me as he tells me to stand taller, but not too tall, to hold myself as though I belong ... but not in such a way that I seem overly-confident.

Everything he says seems like a contradiction to whatever comes out of his mouth next, and it isn't long before frustration starts to get the better of me.

"You have to be subtle in your seduction," he says, waving a dismissive hand at me as his eyes move over the garden. "Try again."

Biting back my irritation, I try my best to do as he says, even though I don't know how to seduce anyone, let alone be subtle in it. Every movement I make, every look I send his way, feels wrong.

"This isn't working," I groan when Eros corrects me yet again, this time on the tone of my voice.

"Try again."

His attention is clearly not on me as I try to repeat the words he tells me, but they are all wrong as they fall from my lips. They lack the charm they held when dripping from his own.

I turn away from him, my hands clenching at my sides. This is clearly a waste of all of our time. I can't do this.

I am a farm girl; what grace and charm I have come in the form of painting and quiet moments with those I love. Not coquettish looks and honeyed words.

I was a fool to think this would ever work. There's absolutely no way I can learn to harness this allure that Eros keeps referring to in time.

"Come," Eros says, pushing himself away from the tree suddenly, "I have an idea."

It's only now that I realize, in his distracted state, that

Eros has forgotten to say anything to Death. Resisting the urge to glance over at Death, I follow Eros, unwilling to draw attention to him and to shatter whatever strange peace has fallen over the two of them.

Eros doesn't even look back to make sure I'm following as we move deeper into the overgrown garden. I'm distracted by the wildness of it all, once more longing to have a paintbrush in my hands and a blank canvas before me.

Pushing into a hidden clearing, Eros stops before a small pool. The surface of the water glimmers, reflecting the vines overhead in an almost mirror-like way.

"Sit," Eros tells me, settling onto the grass beside it and patting the ground next to him.

Hesitantly, I obey.

Flinching as he leans toward me, but instead of touching me, he just points down to the water.

"Look," he says. "Watch yourself; pretend that you are trying to draw yourself over with a single look."

I frown as I turn my attention toward my reflection and try to do as he says. I almost laugh at my attempt. I look absolutely ridiculous just trying to be seductive.

It's clear as day that I have no idea what I'm doing.

"Try again, but widen your eyes and part your lips slightly."

I do as he says, but it does little to make me look any more natural. Before I can say as much, though, he gives me another expression to try.

Watching myself, I have to fight back the urge to cringe. I look so unnatural, so unlike myself, that I'm not sure how anyone could find this pretty, let alone seductive.

"No, not like this," Eros says, mimicking my expression. "Like this."

I stare at him in shock, once again surprised by how well he's able to copy me without ever having seen my face.

"I think you're better at mimicking me than I am you," I say with a sigh. "Perhaps you should be the one seducing Cerberus instead of me."

My comment doesn't get the reaction I'd hoped as Eros instructs me to try again. This time, a pout.

My face refuses, and I look more like I've just stubbed my toe than anything. Frustration tugs at me as I frown down into the water.

"Close your eyes, mortal. Try using what I taught you yesterday."

I glance at Eros' reflection beside me in the pool. Hesitantly, I take a deep breath and close my eyes.

"Feel the emotion you are attempting to use. Harness the energy you are trying to draw to you," he says, his voice warm and comforting.

I bite my tongue as I try to make myself understand his words, but they mean nothing to me. Not when I'd felt it by accident yesterday.

My mind races as I remember how I'd felt in my old life. What drawing attention to me had gotten me in the way of my stepfamily ... and all hope drains out of me.

How could I ever want to harness a power that only draws the attention of people like that?

"Focus."

"I'm trying," I snap before letting out a frustrated sigh.

I'm not back at my father's house. My stepbrother is not waiting in the next room to corner me, I remind myself. Still, it takes a moment for my shoulders to relax.

"Paint a picture of what you want to accomplish in your head."

Sighing, I try my best, but I have no idea how to picture seduction. I'm not even sure how it truly feels, so how am I supposed to paint a picture of it in my head?

My mind spins as I struggle to make this work ... Until my thoughts turn to Death.

I can see him so perfectly, and my heart skips a beat in my chest.

I imagine the way he pulls on his leather gloves. The way he strode through the halls of his palace, his cloak swishing around his feet.

The way he would sit and watch me eat, his eyes never once straying from my face. The dance of his shadows around him when he was particularly amused by something or the softening of his eyes when he looked at my paintings.

How his hands were so gentle with me ... The feel of his lips when they pressed against mine and how perfectly they fit there.

It doesn't take much for me to paint a full picture of him in my mind, and suddenly, it makes sense.

Where Eros drips lust and desire, Death is something else.

He is a force. He is unadulterated power.

He is life, even in death.

He could consume my entire world, and I would let

him if he would but have me. Desire takes on a completely different meaning when I think of him.

It's all-consuming to picture what we could become; of what awaits us if we were to come together.

Opening my eyes, I glance down at the water to find my reflection has been replaced with that of Death's mask. I blink once before realizing that he's come to stand behind me.

Our eyes meet, and I understand what Eros meant earlier. I know the feeling I want to convey more than anything. My entire body burns with it, and I no longer have to question how I want my face to look or how to hold my body. In this moment, I know exactly what I want, and so it seems, does my very being.

Death holds my gaze a moment longer as I gather every ounce of this feeling that I can muster.

I don't stop myself from imagining what it would feel like to be claimed by him. To welcome him into my bed, and it hits me just how desperately I want that to happen. What I would do to give in to him fully.

My emotions course through me as we stare into each other's souls, neither of us moving. I feel awake in ways I never imagined before, suddenly aware of the depth of my feelings ...

Longing for someone like I never have before.

"There," Eros says excitedly. "That. That is how it is done!"

His voice snaps me back to reality, and I blink, my cheeks flaming as I drop Death's gaze. Tears burn my eyes as I force myself to glance at Eros.

For just a moment, I let myself fall too deeply into my

emotions. Reality and fantasy were blurred for one glorious moment. Eros grins, seemingly oblivious to the sting of tears behind my eyes.

"How do you know?" I ask.

Eros' grin widens.

"It is impossible not to know, dear mortal. The very air is heavy with your presence, your desire. This is *exactly* what will win Cerberus over."

"Oh."

"Remember this power. Use it," Eros tells me. "Keep practicing it every chance you get. Try it on anyone and everyone that you come across. You have my permission to practice on any being within my palace at your discretion."

I snort, my hands flying to my mouth a moment too late. Shaking my head, I start to protest, but Eros stops me with a hand on my shoulder.

"That was not a suggestion. It was an order."

"I don't think I can, though."

"You can and you will," he replies with a wave of his free hand. "I am telling you to bring anyone into your bed unless that is what you wish. I am simply telling you to hone your power."

"You're right. I will try."

"I am, and you will. By the time you must be tested, I want you able to bring anyone to their knees with nothing more than a glance. Then, and only then, can I be certain that Cerberus stands no chance against you."

I frown. Surely, this is just an exaggeration. I've only just started to figure this out, and even then, the only reason I've made any progress is because of Death.

I don't know how I will survive if I have to go about constantly thinking of him in such a light.

"Eros—"

He cuts me off by raising his hand abruptly, suddenly turning toward a thick set of overhanging vines. Eros cocks his head to one side as if listening for something.

For a moment, nothing happens, and then a slow smile spreads across his face as he rises to his feet.

"Ah, Persephone. To what do we owe the pleasure of your company?"

30

HAZEL

A moment passes before Persephone slowly steps into view. I'd almost swear her beauty seems to have doubled since last I saw her, further enhanced by the flowers and foliage of the garden.

She gives us a soft smile as she smooths down the silks of her dress, tiny flowers stitched into it with bright threads and intricate beadwork. I can't help but notice how much she seems to belong here amidst the beauty of nature.

Again, my fingers itch to capture this moment on a canvas.

"Hello," she greets us with another soft smile that doesn't quite reach her eyes.

Something seems off as she takes another step closer to us, and I try to pinpoint what it is. She holds herself stiffer than she did when we first met, her eyes harder as she takes us in. Persephone nods once to Death, but her eyes fail to meet his before returning to Eros.

"Might we have a word?"

He nods, "Of course."

"In private, please."

Eros stiffens slightly at this, tilting his head slightly as if he's having a hard time trying to read her. Finally, he gives her a nod, excusing himself in a soft murmur that I barely catch before gesturing to Persephone to follow him away from the pool.

I watch after them as they disappear into the lush greenery around us.

Alone with Death, a heavy silence falls, and I sneak a tentative glance at him from the corner of my eye, unsure what to do. It feels as though there are suddenly too many unspoken things between us. Too many words and too much pain for me to know where to begin.

Though, I suppose in our case, perhaps some things are better left unsaid.

The silence stretches, growing heavier with each passing moment, until Death clears his throat, stepping closer as I feel his eyes slip to me.

"If it would help, you may practice what Eros has taught you on me, little one."

My heart skips a beat in my chest before it sets off racing, threatening to kill me without a moment's notice. I fight the flush I feel creeping over me, my mouth dry as I try to find my voice.

I try to remind myself that he's only being friendly. That this is just his way of helping protect me. He does not feel the same way I do toward him.

Still, these thoughts are all but forgotten as he takes another step toward me.

His eyes search my face as I look up at him, and I struggle to remind myself that this is just part of his promise. He simply wants me to escape the Underworld, to ease his guilt over taking my soul … just as much as I wish my heart didn't beat so hard for him.

"Yes," I finally manage, my voice barely more than a whisper as he offers his hand out to me.

Pulling me to my feet, our eyes meet, and for a moment, I think I've lost the ability to breathe, much less think.

Accepting his offer was a mistake. I don't know how I'll manage with him staring down at me like this, but it almost gives me hope that there's still a shred of feeling left between us.

Despite the growing evidence that there isn't.

"Very well," he says, clearing his throat again. "You may begin when you are ready."

"Okay," I breathe, forcing my eyes away from his.

Staring down at the strange pool, I try to refocus myself as I close my eyes. Prepared for another struggle, I'm surprised by how easily it comes to me this time.

There is no fight to find the right emotions; they're already on the surface, desperate for me to return to them. Somehow, they feel stronger as I reach for them, more certain as I wrap them around myself like armor.

I know exactly what I want.

Who I want.

Opening my eyes, I don't bother looking for my own reflection. Instead, I find his, and I swear I feel our souls crash together through the shimmering water. I hold onto this, letting the power of my emotions build with each beat of my heart ...

Until my desire for him is all-consuming, all-powerful in its intensity.

I turn toward him, my breath catching in my throat as I meet his gaze face to face, and I'm thrown off-balance by what I find within it.

Within *him*.

Without thinking, I take a step back, my stomach dropping out beneath me. Time slows as I fall backward over the edge of the pool. Inky tendrils reaching for me as Death's eyes widen in panic.

"Haz—"

But then his voice is lost to me as I squeeze my eyes shut and sink below the surface.

At first, I find the water to be warm and welcoming as it wraps around me, dragging me deeper and deeper. Only, as I struggle to open my eyes, I realize it isn't water but something much thicker. It weighs me down, and I find myself panicking as I try and fail to get my bearings.

I cry out, but the viscous liquid fills my mouth instead. I can't pull myself free from the pool's hold on me. No matter how hard I try, I cannot reach the surface, and my lungs burn with need.

I can't help but wonder if this is what Death meant about his touch. That I'm not limited to just one death after all.

What would it mean for me, for my body and soul, if I were to die here again?

My body stills, my heartbeat slowing to a dull thrum ...

I'm going to drown.

I'm going to die again without having told Death that I love him.

Just as I think it's all over, strong arms wrap around my waist, and I feel myself being dragged up, up, up, until the water releases its hold on me, and I finally break the surface.

I cough, the thick liquid pouring out of me as a hand cups my cheek, brushing a thumb across my eyes to free them of the water's weight.

Slowly, I open them as the last drops fall from my lashes, and I'm able to see again.

At least, I think I can.

I can't make sense of the being standing before me, dripping gold and glittering like diamonds in the light as it stands waist-deep with me in the pool.

Still keeping one arm around me, the figure reaches up to pull off a mask of molten gold and tosses it aside.

Death.

His beauty somehow more striking as it drips with golden light.

Our eyes meet, and my heart thuds in my chest.

"You saved me," I gasp.

"I would rather die a thousand deaths than see you parted from me again, little one."

I frown in confusion, his words making my mouth go dry. I must have misheard or still have some of this strange water in my ears.

"That can't be right," I breathe as I stare up at him in bewilderment.

"Why not?" he asks, making me realize that I spoke my thought aloud.

"Because ... because of what you told Eros yesterday. About your feelings for me."

His brow furrows as he searches my face as if he's already forgotten what he said. Unable to stop myself, I softly repeat the words that shattered my heart yesterday, dropping my eyes as I say them.

Death stiffens as his arms tighten around me.

Slowly, he reaches out to tilt my chin up so that our eyes meet once again, his own filled with anguish as he looks at me.

"That is not what I meant, little one. I was speaking of his crassness. My feelings for you cannot be summed up in such a way. Eros is mistaken because I adore you. From the day you stumbled into my forest, I have wanted to worship you with every fiber of my being ... and yet, I have found myself unworthy of you."

Blinking, I try to ignore the way my heart beats faster and faster, hardly daring to believe what he's telling me. Fearing that, perhaps, I'm hearing him wrong. And yet, I cannot stop hope from blossoming in my chest as he traces my cheek with his thumb.

"Hazel, my heart beats for you and you alone," Death says, his voice low and gentle. "If you will but have me."

"I will," I say, my voice so soft it's nearly inaudible. "I love you more than I ever dared to let myself believe possible."

Without thinking, without hesitating to consider what I'm doing, I reach up to touch his face.

I take in the sharp planes of his face, my fingers

brushing against his cheek before he has a chance to pull away. Ice shoots through my fingertips, racing up my arm and striking the very depths of my being.

It dawns on me what I've just done as both Death, and I remain frozen in place.

I've touched Death.

I want to curse myself for being so careless, for ending this moment between us, as I search his eyes in panic. Only death doesn't come for me.

A heartbeat passes before I realize his fingers are in my hair, intertwining themselves in the strands at the nape of my neck. His grip tightens on me as something new sparks to life in his eyes.

Before I can question it, he bends to brush his lips against mine, his kiss soft and feather-light as heat and ice mix into passion.

This time, as he pulls me closer to him, his kiss brings me back to life.

31

DEATH

I tremble, hardly daring to believe it possible as I lose myself completely to her. Hazel's touch, the burn of her skin, the press of her lips against mine.

Nothing exists outside of us, and this moment, as we melt into one another, and I deepen our kiss before pulling back.

I take in her beauty as I lift one hand to my mouth and pull off my glove, tossing it aside with a jerk of my head.

"May I?" I whisper, my fingertips hovering next to her face.

"Yes."

Tentatively I trace the line of her jaw toward her chin, and for the first time in my life, I touch someone I love without having to watch them die. My heart shatters, and I have to choke back the tears that burn the backs of my eyes as this realization overwhelms me.

How long I have waited for a moment like this, and to find it here, with her ... I bend, finding her lips with mine, yet again. Hungry for her as I pull her flush against me. Hazel returns my kiss, her heat singeing me as my fingers tighten in her hair.

Gently, I break away, pulling her head to one side as I trail kisses down her neck, savoring the way my fingertips are able to trace the lines of her back. She lets out a small sigh, her body arching into my touch.

I want nothing more than to show her the pleasure she is silently begging me for, but I force myself to go slow. To not rush this moment that I have spent an eternity waiting for.

Putting her arms around my neck, I bend to pick her up so that her legs wrap around my waist as I wade toward the edge of the pool. Her fingers trail up into my hair as I shower her neck and shoulder with tender kisses.

Setting Hazel down on the stone trim, I move to step back, but her legs tighten around me, anchoring me to her. I let out a low growl of want, unable to suppress the surge of possessive want that burns through me at this. A fierce need to finally claim her as mine.

But even as I allow myself a moment to revel in the heat and passion between us, a cold fear grips me.

I know that our love is forbidden. That it goes against everything our worlds stand for. I am a being of darkness, and she is a creature of light.

Our love is not supposed to exist, and yet, here we are, consumed by it ... tempting the Fates with our sheer impossibility.

And I only want her more for it.

Moving to cup the back of her head in one hand, I

lean in to kiss her again as my other trails up her arm, finding the strap of her dress. Only before I can remove it, Hazel's body stiffens, and I pull back just as Eros pushes his way back into the clearing, looking more irate than I have ever seen him.

With a sigh, I remove myself from Hazel. Reaching for my glove, I pull it back on with my teeth before grabbing my mask and refitting it, all too aware of Hazel's sigh as she watches me.

Lifting myself up out of the water, I watch as the strange liquid drips from us both, pooling beneath us like oil before it slowly makes its own way back to join the rest.

I frown as I watch it go, wondering what exactly we just drenched ourselves in.

"What is wrong?" I ask, realizing Eros has yet to address us as he presses his fingertips into his temples

"There has been a change in plans."

Immediately, I am on edge. Narrowing my gaze, I watch as his eyes dart about the small clearing we are standing in.

He has yet to note any changes in us or that the pool has been disrupted. Eros takes a deep breath, raking a hand back through his hair as he shakes his head.

Something is very wrong here.

"What kind of change?" I demand.

"Hades means to leave the Underworld," he says, hesitating before adding, "tomorrow."

"He means to do what?" I growl through clenched teeth.

Eros lets out a frustrated groan, and for the first time

since coming here, it seems we are on the same page. Hazel glances between us, her eyes wide in question as she searches my face for some explanation.

"What does that mean?" she finally asks. "Is that not a good thing for us?"

I shake my head, almost unable to meet her eye, but I force myself to.

She frowns up at me before glancing at Eros. He remains silent, apparently preferring that I deliver the bad news to her. Not that this surprises me.

"If Hades leaves, then it is over for us. Over before we have even had a chance to begin," I tell her.

"Why?"

"If Hades leaves, even if we manage to gain Cerberus' favor, the gates to the Underworld will freeze over. Making it impossible for any soul to pass through them. Making it impossible for you to leave, little one."

She blinks at me, sorrow pouring into me through her gaze for a moment. Then she shakes her head, once again glancing toward where Eros sulks.

"There must be something we can do," she says.

Eros hesitates, finally lifting his head to look our way.

"There might still be a way, but—"

"Tell us," I demand of him. "Immediately, we have no time to waste."

He frowns. "I do not know if it will work…"

"Eros, out with it," I growl as I start to lose patience with him.

"We could attempt to convince Hades to stay," Eros says, shrugging as he glances in my general direction.

I snort at his suggestions.

"Do not play games with me, Eros. What possible reason could we give Hades to make him stay?"

"Hazel."

A heavy silence falls at this, and I cannot help but glance down at her, where she still sits at the edge of the pool, her eyes wide as she glances between us.

"What the hell are you talking about?" I ask carefully.

"He is hosting a masquerade tonight as a sort of final farewell. Hazel could attempt to convince him. To seduce him into staying here."

"No," I growl, rage clenching my heart at the thought of him touching her. "Absolutely not."

Eros shakes his head at me before snapping, "And do you have a better suggestion? Any other plans we could attempt?"

"What about Persephone?" Hazel asks.

"I would not concern yourself with her," Eros says with a bitter laugh. "It is no secret that Hades has grown cold to her. He has had his fill of her, apparently ... but you, Hazel, are a prized possession among mortal souls. You could be just the thing to bring him back to life, so to speak. And then, steal the key before he is any the wiser. Assuming she learns where it is, first."

"No. I will not allow it. We will find another way, one that does not involve her going anywhere near Hades, let alone seducing him."

I watch as Eros shakes his head at me. While he might think I am being thick-headed, I think he is too quick to risk Hazel's safety.

He is trying to find the easiest solution here, one that involves what he knows best. But I know the sort of destruction that man could rack on someone like her. I will not stand for it.

All we need is a little more time.

"I am all ears, Death, if you have any better plans," Eros mutters, slumping against a tree.

I give myself a moment to think.

Eros lets out a sigh, obviously mistaking my silence as me giving in. I am not about to quit that easily, though. Not when it involves Hazel going before the God of the Underworld.

There has to be another way.

We just have to find it.

"So?" Eros presses.

"I do not know," I admit. "I need more time—"

"That is the only thing we do not have. It is now or never. This may be your only chance."

I hate that he is right, but there is nothing I can do about it.

"What do you suggest then?" I ask.

"Practice," Eros says, turning his attention to Hazel. "This will be your greatest challenge yet. With so little time left to practice, we cannot afford to waste a single moment."

"Okay."

I give him a nod, my shadows swirling in frustration, as I glance down at Hazel. She looks nervous, her face paling and her eyes widening as she takes in what is being asked of her.

I wish I could reach out and comfort her. That I could think of some other way to get us out of here without involving Hades in such a way.

In any way.

"One last thing, as much as I hate to do this, we need to add a new rule," Eros says with a sigh. "No one is to go so far as to actually ... satiate Hazel before she attempts to seduce Hades."

"Why would you say that?" Hazel nervously asks as I eye him warily.

Eros grins at us, licking his lips as though he can taste something in the air, and I suddenly realize he can probably taste us. The desire that burned between us. How close I came to losing myself in her before he arrived.

"Whatever happened between the two of you while I was gone has awakened something in Hazel that even Hades will be unable to resist. We cannot afford to have that amount of desire quelled with satiation before she faces him."

32

HAZEL

A sly grin splits Eros' face as he glances between us, leaving me feeling exposed. Even without sight, it's as though he can sense what happened between us.

"So, what exactly did the two of you get up to while I was away?" Eros asks.

"That is no concern of yours, Eros," Death replies coldly.

"See, that is where you are wrong," he snorts. "That is *exactly* my concern. I need to know how best to intensify her allure, and whatever the two of you did seems to have done just the trick."

"We kissed," I say as Death falls quiet, clearly unwilling to share the details of what happened between us. Not that I want to either, but what choice do we have?

"You kissed?" Eros asks, blinking in surprise. "Kissed, how exactly?"

My cheeks burn as I search for the words to explain what happened, but I am saved from having to do so as

Death speaks up. He gives Eros just enough details to paint a simple picture of how I fell in the pool, and we ended up discovering we could touch.

Eros' brow furrows as he listens, stepping absent-mindedly toward the pool. He stops just short of it, crouching to dips his fingers into the strange water within.

Shaking his head, he chuckles to himself.

"I should have known," he says, rising to his feet. "Leave it to my brother to have a pool of longing in the middle of his private gardens."

"A what?" I ask, watching as the liquid coats the tips of his fingers.

"If touched, the liquid will quite literally cling to those who long for another. Mostly harmless stuff, though it can become dangerous enough to drown you should your longing be too great ... and you happen to fall into it."

I don't understand how that has to do with Death and I being able to touch."

"It may or may not have anything to do with it, but it is very possible that falling into it created enough of a barrier between the two of you to be able to touch."

I nod as if this makes any sense to me.

"And what about the longing?"

My question apparently isn't as subtle as I thought by the way Eros grins at this. He crouches down again and plunges his hand into the liquid, his head tilted slightly, as he glances in my direction.

"It does not create longing, only reveals it. True longing, that is."

I watch as the liquid slowly climbs up his arm, not unlike the way I've seen Death's veins grow inky in his fury. The gold trails over his skin, spreading across his chest and up his neck and half his face before he pulls his hand out.

He looks down at the gold vining up his body before slowly lifting his pale eyes to mine. My breath catches in my throat as I realize what he's telling me, and then, he rises and shakes the liquid from it. I can't help but watch as it glides over the ground to collect once more in the mirrored pool, as if it had never left.

Eros snaps his fingers, drawing my attention away from the shimmering water and back to him.

"All right, there is no time to lose. We have ... three, perhaps four hours left to practice before twilight."

"Why twilight?"

"Because pools of longing are known to be far too powerful to mess with at night, and we must have time to prepare for the masquerade. Now, are you ready to get back in the pool?"

"What?" Death and I ask together.

My eyes slide back to the still waters at this. Even now, it looks so harmless, but I suppose that should serve as a lesson to me about this place.

Nothing is as innocent as it appears.

"Get back in the pool," Eros repeats. "Unless Death is willing to test his touch on you outside the water."

"No," Death answers without hesitation.

Eros seems unsurprised by this, but I get the feeling I've missed something important as my gaze shifts between them.

"I don't understand. Why do we need to get back in the pool at all?"

"You do not *have* to, as long as you are then willing to let me practice on you instead."

"Why is physical touch necessary at all, Eros?" Death cuts in. "She is only meant to be charming them into getting what we need, not taking them to bed."

"First, because it is the fastest way to ignite desire, if done right. Second, because even I cannot say how far seduction may lead. Especially with Hades."

Eros flinches as Death lets out a low guttural growl at this last part, and I shudder as I realize what he means.

They can't possibly think I would go so far as to ... no. Not with Hades.

"I am simply saying it is a possibility," Eros says quickly. "We must be prepared for everything at this point. And then, of course, there may still be Cerberus to deal with."

I realize as he says this that he may not be wrong. I hadn't thought of that possibility before, nor do I know if I am capable of going to such extents even to free myself from this place. Would it be worth it if it led to me getting my life back and the chance of a future with the man that I love?

"Do you actually mean for me to lie with Hades?"

Peeking up at Death, I can see that he's none too thrilled by this either.

"Only if absolutely necess—" Eros starts.

"No," Death growls. "Regardless of it being a possibility, I will not allow that to happen, little one."

"We still need her to be prepared for tonight, whatever happens," Eros says.

"Fine, but you will press no further than she is comfortable with."

"Then it is settled. Shall we begin?"

"Right now?" I ask.

"Yes, but let us start with something simple. Can you dance, mortal?"

"Again. Drop your gaze and slowly circle him," Eros instructs.

I let out a frustrated sigh as I do what he says. We've spent the better part of two hours practicing several dances, looks, and light touches that I'm meant to use on Hades. Apparently, getting back in the pool isn't necessary if you're such a terrible dancer that it stresses out the God of Desire for you.

The excitement I had felt earlier about being able to touch Death has evaporated with Eros hovering around us critiquing, our every move.

Well, *my* every move.

"Try again," Eros says. "Like this."

I step aside as Eros takes my place and shows me what he's trying to get me to do. Death stiffens as the pale god steps around him, mimicking how I should trail my fingers over my partner's body. How I should glance up at him before quickly looking away. How I should press my body ...

"Enough," Death growls, shoving Eros away from him

when he gets a little too close. "How is this helping anyone but yourself?"

"You would know if the mortal was doing it right," Eros retorts, signaling for me to try again.

Sighing, I step toward Death and slowly lift my gaze to his. The moment that our eyes meet, it's as if everything else falls away. As if by magic, we step together and I'm swept away from the present back to the ballroom where it's once again just the two of us.

A small smile pulls at the corners of my lips as I move closer, circling him as I run my hand lightly across his chest and then back to return once again. I meet his eyes once more before dipping my head away shyly.

"Turn your back to him as you step closer," Eros orders distantly, and this time I don't hesitate.

I turn, and Death's hands wrap around my waist to pull me flat against his body. Immediately, I can feel the heat ignite between us as one of his hands moves up the center of my body to grab my neck, gently pulling it to one side as he dips his masked face to the exposed skin there.

"Finally," Eros interrupts with a loud, slow clap. "That is it. That is what you have to bring to the ball. Hades will stand no chance."

The reminder that Eros is watching us is enough to have me stepping away as Death shoots a murderous look his way. Eros is crouched by the pool, an arm's length away from us, frowning down into the water.

"I just need you to maintain that level of desire."

"Maybe I could if you didn't keep interrupting," I answer.

"Or perhaps you need more hands-on instruction," Eros says, leaning forward to dip his fingers in the pool.

That's all it takes for his face to shift. Gone is his frustration with us, replaced by desire as it burns in his gaze. He stands and reaches for me before I realize what's happening.

"Eros," Death warns, but our host doesn't listen as he drops his lips to mine. Before he can kiss me, though, Death reacts.

I am pulled back against Death's chest just as he kicks Eros square in the middle of his. I let out a cry of surprise as I watch Eros disappear beneath the metallic glint of the water.

I wait for him to resurface, prepared for him and Death to throw themselves at each other.

Except, he doesn't resurface.

"Death," I say, my panic growing as I look up at him. "Save him!"

I can't even make out Eros' form within the pool, but I don't have to in order to know what's happening. He's caught in his own longing as it slowly drowns him. Death lets out a deep sigh before releasing me and jumping into the pool.

Wading through the water, he reaches for Eros, tugging him back to the surface before depositing him on the edge of the pool. Crumpled in a heap, Eros coughs and gasps for air as thick golden liquid splatters on the ground.

"Eros, are you okay?" I ask, tentatively reaching out to place a hand on his shoulder but pulling back as he flinches away from my touch.

His eyes seem to clear for just a moment as he stares down at the ground. Gold streaks staining his otherwise pale skin and hair. Then he pulls himself up, the liquid dripping from him and finding its way back to the pool.

"That is enough for today."

"But today is all we have."

"She is ready," Eros snaps. Then, with little more than a glance toward us, the pale god excuses himself.

I watch as he disappears into the gardens before turning to Death.

"What was that?" I ask.

"What?"

Annoyance flares in me as I stare at him. I'd rather not spend what little time we have remaining before the masquerade arguing, but I hate the way his eyes flash as he stares down at me.

"Would you have let him drown if I hadn't asked you to save him?"

Death hesitates before answering, "Yes."

"Why?"

"He is consumed by his own longing for you—"

"So, what if Eros longs for me? Is that enough of a reason to let him die?"

"Of course not. But...."

"But nothing. You are not to harm Eros simply because he desires me, is that understood? If anything, you should be thankful for him."

"Thankful," Death scoffs. "Why the hell would I be thankful for that?"

"Because without him, we may never have come together here."

Death is quiet for a long moment before he lets out a deep sigh. He looks away for a moment before nodding his head slowly, his eyes returning to mine.

"You are right, little one," he says, his eyes burning with desire as he reaches for my hand from the edge of the pool. "These feelings for you are powerful, and I have not yet learned to fully control them. I want you. I desire no one but you, and I would rather kill than see someone with you. Not before I have yet to know you fully myself."

With that, Death pulls me gently into the pool with him, carrying me in his arms as he wades deeper. Setting me on my feet, he pulls off his mask before we both slip beneath the surface.

Rising back up out of the water, Death cups my face, tilting my head back as he bends to press his lips to mine. Immediately, I'm lost in his kiss. I need more, want more.

I reach for him, pressing my body to his as my hands work to loosen his shirt.

He lets out a low chuckle that rumbles through me, deepening our kiss just as I manage to pull out the hem. My hand slips beneath, feeling the strength of his cold body as they trace lower.

"Hazel," he growls deeply when my hand slips to his belt.

"Please," I whisper, even as he reaches to pull my hand away.

"Not yet, little one. Some things cannot be undone, and I would have you safe first."

He starts to step back just as I reach up to pull aside one of the dress' straps, my heart thundering in my chest as he freezes. My fingers dip below the plunging neckline as I trace it lower, fully intending to let him see more of me. Wanting him to.

"Hazel," he says again, his voice tighter as he quickly reaches to stay my hand. "Please. I cannot say what I would do."

His eyes linger on my breast, still barely concealed beneath thin layers of fabric, before lifting to meet mine.

"Then do not say it," I say, but his hand tightens around my wrist, refusing to allow me to show him more.

"You will know me, but not yet. Not before the masquerade. Once this is all over, I promise to finish what we have started."

Chills of anticipation race across my skin at this, and I finally relinquish my attempts to have him take me here and now. I release the dress strap, and Death catches it to slip it safely back over my shoulder.

"Come, it is time for us to prepare for a ball," he says, pressing one last soft kiss to my lips before once again donning his mask.

33

HAZEL

All too soon, we're returning to Eros' bedroom to prepare for the night ahead.

I'm all nerves as we're greeted by the two female attendants from before.

"Come," says the one who's been helping me, "you must be bathed."

I follow her into the bathroom, reluctant to leave Death's side even as I see the other woman hand him his old set of clothes and lead him behind a partition.

"What is your name?" I ask when the attendant shuts the door behind us and begins preparing the bath for me.

"My name?" she repeats, apparently taken aback by my question. "I ... I do not remember ever having a name."

I stare at her for a long moment waiting for her to continue, but she remains silent, her eyes downcast. I can't help but feel a pang of sympathy for her. I know all too well what it can feel like to lose one's identity to those you serve, to feel like you simply exist without a purpose of your own.

"Would you like me to give you name?"

She looks up at me, her eyes wide as she pours a bottle of pink liquid into the bath.

"You would do that for me?"

"If you wish it."

"I would like that very much," she says, nearly unable to contain her excitement as she watches me.

I chew my lip as I try to think of a name to give her, suddenly finding my mind as blank as a new canvas. I'm starting to worry I won't be able to come up with a name when one suddenly pops into my head.

"How about Florence?"

"Florence," she repeats, testing out the name for herself. "Yes. Yes, I think that will do."

I give her a smile as she rises and helps me out of my dress.

"Thank you, Florence," I say, sinking into the steaming bath, and she beams at me.

Florence sets to work washing my body and hair, taking extra care to message my head and shoulders too. Once satisfied that I'm as clean and relaxed as she can get me, Florence helps me up out of the bath.

Wrapping a towel around me, she leads me over to the chair by the fire. I'm barely able to sit still as the attendant rubs sweetly-scented oils into my skin and pulls my hair into an elaborate crown of braids that hangs down my back.

It's only when she finishes that I realize I don't see a dress set out for me.

"I'm not going naked, am I?" I whisper to her in fear.

"No," she chuckles, "Eros insisted he present the dress to you personally once you were ready."

With that, she turns and walks over to open the door. Eros stands just outside, and in his arms is the sparkling white gown I'd wanted to wear earlier.

"You will wear this tonight," he says, "and put all others to shame."

My eyes widen as I take in his gift. Standing, I clutch the towel to me as I reach out hesitantly, my fingers grazing the fabric. It's soft and cool to the touch, and I can feel the weight of it in my hands. It's truly a work of art as it sparkles like starlight.

"Thank you," I say softly as Florence accepts the dress for me.

"Thank me by wearing it and winning your safety."

I nod, hardly knowing what to say, as he gives me a nod and excuses himself from the room.

Florence helps me into the dress, and it is as if it was made specifically for me. I catch a glimpse of myself in the mirror and can hardly believe it is me staring back.

The sparkling white fabric hugs my curves in all the right places, with a fitted bodice and low-cut neckline that shows off just enough of my cleavage to be alluring without being vulgar.

Florence places a pair of opalescent heels on the floor, carefully helping me step into them to complete the outfit.

I feel like a princess, though I know that this is far from a fairytale.

Still, I smile as Florence opens the door, and I step out

into the main room where Death and Eros are waiting. The skirt falls in gentle folds around my legs, sweeping the floor with every step I take.

"Perfect," Eros says quietly. "Your presence is ... everything."

I flush at his praise, taking in the intricate design of his own bright white garments and ornate mask. They almost seem to float around him while at the same time fitting him like a glove. My eyes shift behind him as Death steps forward, emerging from his own shadows.

He is wearing his own clothes now and is obviously much more comfortable for it. He stands tall and imposing as his eyes slowly move over me, causing the fire I feel for him to burn brighter within me.

"Stunning," Death breathes, stepping closer. He reaches out to brush away a stray hair before placing a delicate mask over the top half of my face and tying the ribbons behind my head. "You would outshine even the brightest star in the darkest of nights ... but here, you will blind them. Are you sure you want to do this?"

I look up at him as he searches my face with uncertainty.

I can understand his hesitation right now; after all, we've barely had any time to prepare ... but we've come too far.

Just a matter of hours now, and we'll see if I can manage to catch Hades' eye. Hopefully, all I need to do is to intrigue him enough to delay his departure from the Underworld long enough for Cerberus to return ... or to get my hands on the gate key.

Surely, I can do that.

"As ready as I can be."

Death looks ready to call the whole thing off, but Eros is quick to sweep in as he offers me his arm. It's enough to have Death pushing him aside to do the same. I slip my arm around Death's and give Eros a grateful smile as we move past him.

My nerves are on edge the whole way to Hades' palace, my mind spinning with a million and one ways tonight could play out.

Reaching the main road, we pause in the dark alleyway, and I watch as beings dressed in extravagant outfits walk past us toward the towering sapphire palace.

"Come, let us join them before we are late," Eros says, stepping out into the crowd. Death and I follow behind him, and I blush deeply as I hear their gasps and questioning whispers. It would appear, even among a crowd of masked beings, Death's presence stands out.

"It is you, little one," Death says as if reading my mind. "You who they whisper about, not me."

"The battle is already half-won," Eros whispers as he turns to lean in between us. Reaching the top of the stairs, we make our way into the sparkling palace, this time unhindered by stone guards. It's only when we draw near to the main ballroom that I feel my arm slip, and turning, I realize both Eros and Death are nowhere to be seen amongst the crowd pushing by me.

Panicked, I step toward the ballroom to realize the rest of the guests have already gathered to turn and look at me, only ... it isn't just me they're staring at.

"Hello there," comes a deep voice behind me. "You are a pretty little thing, no?"

Slowly, I turn and look up into Hades' masked face, blue fire burning around the edges. For a moment, every word of Eros' training leaves my mind as I stare up at the man.

Behind him, my eyes catch on Persephone; her head is tilted as she takes me in. Swallowing past my nerves, I quickly pull myself together and drop him a low curtsy.

"Thank you for having me," I say softly, before quickly adding. "My king."

I can feel his eyes lingering on me, and I cautiously lift mine to peek up at him through my lashes, giving him a nervous smile before dropping them again.

He takes a step toward me, his head cocking slightly to one side, and I force myself to pretend I don't notice.

"Excuse me, my king," I say, rising and allowing my skirts to brush against him. Stepping into the crowded ballroom before he can say a word to me, I feel his eyes burning into me as they track me through the room.

Stepping behind a particularly tall couple, I let out a sigh. Somehow, I've already managed to gain his attention. Now, I just have to hope it was enough.

Finding a place near the dance floor, I watch as couples twirl in each other's arms. Suddenly, across the room, through the shifting couples, Hades appears. His eyes find mine, and I allow color to stain my cheeks as I carefully pull my gaze away from his.

But when I next glance up, he's already gone, a mixture of fear and disappointment twisting my stomach.

Trying to ignore this, I turn my focus back to the dancing couples. I'm so distracted watching the colorful dresses as they swish about that I don't notice the presence behind me until it's too late.

Turning, I once again find Hades standing there. His gaze is on the dancers, but I feel his hand slip to the small of my back. When the song ends, he glances down at me.

"Dance with me," he orders.

I nod, and he takes my hand to lead me onto the dance floor. The moment my skin touches his, I feel his full attention shift to me, and I'm thankful he doesn't seem to recognize me as he gives me a questioning look.

The other guests make room for us, watching us out of the corner of their eyes. I'm careful to keep my gaze trained on him, though I'm desperate to search the crowd for signs of Death or Eros.

"You have truly captured my attention tonight," Hades says as the dance begins. "Not an easy task, if I say so myself."

I cringe inwardly at what I'm sure must be a lie as he spins me about the room. I'm suddenly thankful for my lessons as I manage to cling to him, brushing against him just enough that I can feel his growing desire. Pride blossoms in my chest for just a moment as we dance.

Until I notice Persephone standing at the top of a set of stairs, her eyes narrowed as she watches her husband dance with me.

It's clear to everyone now that Hades has chosen me for the night. That he's chasing after me. Guilt knots my stomach painfully as she watches. I can only imagine what she is going through as she takes in the scene before her, knowing she's unable to stop him from choosing to take another to his bed at the end of the night.

"I would have you," Hades whispers into my ear, his breath hot on my neck as he pulls my attention back to him. "I will find you again once the others have left."

With that, he drops his hands from me, and I'm left wondering what to do as I move away from the dance floor.

The last thing I want is to go to him, but what choice do I have? I have won his favor, but for how long? I didn't even have a chance to ask him a single question, let alone find out where he might keep the key to the Underworld.

People and creatures press in as I try to move through them, suddenly feeling more trapped than ever. Overwhelmed, I slip from the ballroom.

The corridor is quiet as I press my back against the cold crystal wall and let out a sigh. I give myself a few seconds before attempting to collect myself.

This is what I want, I remind myself. This is what we needed to happen. Still, I can't help the wariness and regret that overtakes me at the thought of Hades will want from me.

Pushing myself away from the wall, I take a deep breath before starting toward the ballroom again. I barely make it more than a few steps before inky darkness swirls up around me.

Spinning, I watch as Death emerges from the shadows, his eyes burning in their intensity as they remain fixed on me. Without a word, he pulls me to him and presses my back up against the wall once again. He covers my body with his, cloaking us both in shadows as he brings a gloved hand to my face, running his thumb gently over my cheek.

"Let us be done with this," he breathes. "Come away with me, Hazel. Let us find each other in the pool and forget we ever came here. Let me bring down this realm for you."

"We have a plan, Sydian," I whisper, swallowing hard as I try to force myself not to get distracted by how much I want to do just as he says.

"To hell with the plan. To hell with them all," Death growls. "I cannot stand the sight of you with him nor the thought of you giving yourself to him in any way. Please, we can find another way."

Unable to stop myself, I nod. That's all he needs before he grabs my hand and pulls me away from the wall and down the corridor. We say nothing as we slip through the palace, my heels echoing off the crystal, we all but run toward the entryway.

"My shoes," I say when I nearly twist my ankle exiting Hades' palace.

"Damn them," Death growls, spinning to bend me over his shoulder while he slips them off and tosses them aside before sweeping me up into his arms. "I'd rather carry you anyway."

Sticking to the shadows of the city, we move through the streets before finally finding our way back to Eros' palace. Death carries me through the golden halls as we make our way back to the pool.

Stopping beside it, Death moves to set me down just as I see a familiar glint of red in his pocket. I don't know what comes over me, but I can't seem to help myself as I reach to pull it out.

My heart thuds in my chest as I stare down at the package tied off with a red ribbon.

"Where did you get this?" I ask, looking up at Death as he stills.

"Hazel, I—"

"Where did you find this?"

"In the forest, where I met you."

"When?"

Death hesitates before answering, "The day I met you."

"And you didn't give it to me?"

"I meant to, but—"

"But you lied about it. You told me you hadn't found it. Why?"

"I ... I could not bear to give you something that reminded you of the love of another man." I shake my head as I take a step back from him, my heart shattering within me as I try to process what he's just said. "Please, Hazel, I never meant to hurt you."

"And yet, you have. Would you separate me from everyone who loves me?" I say, my voice choked as I turn and race out of the garden.

"Hazel, wait!"

I don't stop. I don't look back as I tear through the palace and burst out onto the streets of the strange city. My bare feet ache as they slap against the stone, but still, I don't stop.

Somehow, I make it to the city gates and slip out, disregarding the sound of my name being called out behind me as I sprint off toward the towering forest.

Reaching the edge of the trees, I pause, wariness finally settling over me as I peer into the darkness beyond.

"Hazel, please let me explain," I turn to find Death slowly approaching with his hands held to either side.

My heart aches, and I realize how foolish I have been … and how foolish I would be not to at least let him try. Just as I open my mouth to agree, an enormous white creature suddenly leaps up behind him.

A scream tears from my throat as I take in its huge claws and fangs, and I stumble backward into the trees just as Death glances over his shoulder.

And the next second, I'm lost.

Alone with nothing around me but trees.

No white beast.

No Death.

Blinking, I stumble forward another step before screaming out for Death.

For anyone.

There's no answer.

Panic begins to claw up my throat as I turn, taking in the endless expanse of forest around me. Again, I shout for Death.

Nothing.

Turning back, I dart off into the trees. Surely, he was just behind me. I can find him again.

It's not until I hear a terrifying growl that I switch to run in the opposite direction. I refuse to allow this place or these creatures to claim me.

Not without a fight.

34

EROS

I shift back to my human form as Death turns toward me. Fury rolls off of him in powerful waves as he begins to curse at me.

"Damn you, Eros. I curse you to high heaven and hell; you should have known better than to ever suggest trying to seduce Hades!"

My own anger matches his as I step toward him, meeting him with my own harsh words.

"Me? Fuck you! What the hell were you thinking," I demand as I do my best to get a grip on myself, "stealing Hazel away like that?!"

"This has gone too far, Eros," Death replies.

We are nearly toe to toe at this point, each of us dragging in deep angry breaths. For a moment, I wait for Hazel to interrupt. To push between us as she normally would to separate us.

But no one says anything or stops us from lashing out at one another.

Frowning, I glance about only to realize Hazel is not here.

My anger melts away as fear begins to replace it.

"Where is Hazel?" I ask.

"She is ..." Death starts as he glances about, suddenly realizing that she is not here with us. "She was right in front of me. You scared her off, you fool!"

When he glances at me, the anger in his eyes has been replaced with fear. Fear as terrible as my own. I have never seen Death look so terrified as he does now, and I cannot even enjoy it.

Not when that fear could mean Hazel's life.

"We have to find her," I say. "Now."

Death nods once as I move to shift again.

Leaving my human form behind, I welcome the heightened senses of this form. With my nose in the air, I search for her scent before taking off into the forest after it. I can feel Death following behind me, chasing after her as his shadows crash alongside me.

With each step that she takes, I can sense her shifting to another location. The forest bending and twisting as it helps her evade us and make her escape. This never-ending forest of madness slowly stealing her further and further away.

The Fates themselves would have to be on her side for her to escape here on her own. And knowing them, I fear that there is not enough luck left in all the realms to save her.

I push myself to move faster, determined to get to her before she is lost to us. Death is just behind me the entire way, following at each turn and every change in direction.

With each step, the forest seems more determined than ever to lose her. I will not allow it to steal her away from me.

Suddenly, I sense a shift.

Her scent changes from something pleasant to one reeking of emotion. To something drowned in absolute horror and pain.

She is no longer moving.

Panic flares through me as I turn and bolt off toward her, finally able to hone in on her location.

My heart pounding, I move toward her with all the speed I have, Death trailing just a few seconds behind me.

35

HAZEL

One moment, I'm crashing through the dark forest, and the next, I find myself stumbling out of the tree line just beside the locked gates of the Underworld.

I blink in confusion as I try to make sense of what just happened. I glance about, but I'm alone.

Well, at least alone on this side of the gates.

Cerberus is nowhere to be seen, but on the other side of the gates, my eyes catch on something that has my heart nearly stopping in my chest. I take a step back, attempting in vain to put distance between myself and what I'm looking at.

Souls wander about aimlessly, waiting to be let into the Underworld. They don't seem to notice me as I stand here, chest heaving as I watch them through the gates.

Finally, I brave a step closer, allowing my curiosity to pull me toward them. Wondering if they are as lost as I was when I first arrived.

Searching their faces my gaze suddenly catches as my

heart skips a beat in my chest. Taking another step forward, I freeze, my mind blanking as I try to process what I'm seeing.

It's my father.

My heart goes still in my chest as I watch him wandering about with the other souls. In a blink, I feel as though my entire world has come crumbling down.

Behind me, I can just make out the sounds of a large beast crashing toward me, but I don't care.

I don't even turn to look. I'm too numb to react or do anything but stare at my father's soul. A soul that's still oblivious to my presence on the other side of the gates.

Even as I catch a flash of white out of the corner of my eye as a giant creature bursts out of the dark forest, I don't so much as flinch.

"Kill me," I whisper.

Let me be done with this world of lies.

Turning toward it, I watch as, at the last moment, the beast shifts into the form of Eros. He opens his arms to me, and I stumble toward him, finally breaking out of my trance.

Tears stream down over my cheeks as he catches me, wrapping his arms around me. Eros pulls me close, holding me tightly to his chest as I sob into him. His hands smooth my hair as he attempts to calm me down enough to understand what's happened.

But I fear there is nothing that will ever calm me down after seeing Father here.

"Hazel, what has happened? Did Hades hurt you?"

"No ... he's dead," I sob into his chest, waving a hand at the gate.

Eros glances between me and the souls on the other side, his brow furrowing as he tries to piece together who I'm talking about.

"He's dead," I repeat in between gasps. "My father. He's dead."

The words tumble from my mouth as fresh tears spring to my eyes. My heart feels as though it's being pulled straight from my chest, having given voice to my worst fear.

"Hazel—"

Eros remains quiet as I finally pull away, my eyes narrowing on Death as he steps toward us.

Death didn't save my father.

Instead, Death has stolen everything from me.

36

DEATH

I step from the trees, taking in the scene before me.

It takes a moment for me to understand what I am seeing. That Eros holds Hazel in his arms, her face buried in his chest as she sobs uncontrollably.

It makes no sense to me, and yet, no matter how many times I blink, the scene never changes.

Fury burns within me as I watch him hold her in his arms. Despite wanting to understand why she has sought him out, my anger overwhelms me.

"Hazel—"

Stepping back from Eros, her gaze meets mine. Hazel's rage own rage makes them burn bright as she takes me in.

"Hazel—" I start again, but she silences me with the narrowing of her eyes.

"Stay away from me," she hisses.

"What happened?"

"You lied to me."

I frown at this. I realize I should have told her about

the book, I never meant to keep it from her ... It was but a moment of weakness.

"If this is about the book, I can—"

"My father is dead," she says, pointing toward the gate.

"What?"

My brow furrows as I follow the point of her finger.

Immediately my eyes search out her father's soul as it wanders about on the other side. Waiting for Cerberus to return and allow him to pass through the gate and on to the rest of his eternity.

I straighten slightly as I realize what this must mean.

"You told me your shadows collect souls as an extension of yourself, or is that a lie too?"

"That is true, but ... Hazel, I swear, your father lived," I say carefully. "Our bargain ensured that he would survive what you came to me for, but it did not mean he would live forever. It is possible something happened to him the moment our deal was complete."

The moment the words leave my mouth, I realize my error, and I curse myself for speaking. Have I learned nothing in my years of silence?

Her eyes widen with hurt and grief before narrowing with rage. In this moment, even I know anger is an easier emotion than accepting that death is a part of life. Easier than the grief of a sacrifice made in vain ... or the betrayal of her stepmother, who I am certain is behind her father's untimely death.

"You promised me he would survive," she says, her voice breaking my heart as I watch Hazel's anger morph into unrelenting grief. Unable to stop herself, she turns to look back at where her father stands.

He seems unaware of her attention, or truly anything, as he simply waits for the gates to open.

"Father," Hazel says, stepping toward him. "Please, look at me."

I narrow my eyes as I watch him standing there, unmoved by her pleas. His state makes it almost certain that his death is a final state, his body too far gone to be raised from the dead.

Still, as I watch them, I realize Hazel will not believe me until I can prove to her that I upheld my end of the bargain just as much as she did hers. Prove to her that I did not intentionally mean to hurt her.

I need to find out what happened to him and see how to right this horrendous wrong.

"I will find a way to fix this," I tell her.

She just shakes her head at me, unshed tears brightening her eyes as she turns back to Eros.

My chest tightens at the way he looks at her, and for a beat, she says nothing as she stares up at him.

"Take me to the Judges, please," she begs him quietly. "Let me face my own judgment and be done with this torment."

"No," Eros says, only hesitating for a moment.

I know he is eager to do anything she asks of him, but thankfully it appears he is not fool enough to do that. Bringing her before the Judges would only ensure that she was lost to us for eternity.

"Fine, then leave me here to await Cerberus' return so that he can take me."

"Perhaps we should take a moment before deciding anything," Eros says carefully.

"I want to face them," she argues.

Eros glances at me before saying, "There may still be hope for your father. After all, he has yet to pass through the gate."

I open my mouth to argue but quickly close it.

There is too much that remains unknown, and I cannot promise her anything to do with her father's soul yet. I still do not know exactly what killed him or even the state of his physical body. It is one thing to hope we will be able to return her but to hope the same for her father is … unlikely at best.

Yet as she turns, I see that Eros' words have given her new hope, and I am unable to bring myself to quash it. It might be a fool's errand, but if it buys us time before Hazel demands to be taken before the Judges, then perhaps Eros is smarter than I have given him credit for.

"For now, we must return to my palace so that we can figure out a new plan," Eros says.

Hazel nods, allowing him to gently lead her several steps away from the gate before pulling free. Running over to the gate, she unties the red ribbon around the book and reaches through to grab her father's hand. Pulling him closer, she ties the ribbon around his hand, securing him to the bars.

"To keep him away from the river," she says in answer to Eros' questioning look as they start toward the forest. I move to follow after them, but Hazel turns, stopping me in my tracks with a hard look.

"I want you nowhere near me. I have had enough lies to last me a lifetime. Two lifetimes."

Eros flinches as he glances at me.

I feel my heart crack into a thousand pieces at the anger in her voice, the certainty in her gaze. She truly wants nothing to do with me, believing that I lied.

That I *deceived* her into giving up her soul.

I open my mouth but find there are no words to convince her otherwise.

"Very well," I force myself to say. "If that is truly what you wish."

"It is."

It takes everything in me to remain rooted to the spot.

With that, she turns and allows Eros to guide her away. He shoots me another look of concern, and my heart bleeds for her as I watch them disappear into the forest. No matter how badly I want to storm after Eros or take Hazel in my arms to comfort her, I know that would only make matters worse.

It is a pain unlike anything I've ever felt, knowing she is within reach, but I cannot go to her. Watching a part of me being slowly ripped away from me to never be returned.

I cannot allow that to be the end of us.

I will not.

I have to prove my innocence in this and the depth of my love for her.

Even if I have to go before the Fates themselves to prove it.

THANK YOU

Thank you for reading *Touch of Death*, the second book in the *Tempting the Fates* series.

If you enjoyed this book ...

You can stay up to date on upcoming new releases in this series and others by following Alice Wilde on **Amazon**, **Facebook**, Instagram, or Tiktok, or by signing up for her newsletter at alicewilde.com.

If you would recommend this book, or others by Alice Wilde, please consider leaving a review on Amazon or reaching out to let her know!

ALSO BY ALICE WILDE

Tempting the Fates

Kiss of Death

Touch of Death

Until Death

Love and Death

A Kingdom of Wolves

Of Wolves and Women

Of Wolves and Warriors

Of Wolves and Wives

A Deal with the Devils

The Vampire's Deal

The Vampire's Maiden

The Vampire's Vow

Fated to the Alphas

Alpha Forsaken

Alpha Marked

Alpha Claimed

Alpha Bound

The White Wolf Trilogy

Pack Lies

Pack Mates

Pack Alpha

The Royal Shifters

Her Betrothal

Her Highlander

Her Viking

Her Warrior

Her Prophecy

The Shifters of Africa

The Lioness of Egypt

The Pride of Egypt

The Queen of Egypt

Quick Reads

My Cup of Tea

The Christmas Wish

ABOUT THE AUTHOR

Alice Wilde works as a full-time game editor, graphic designer, and, most importantly, author.

She loves creating paranormal, fantasy romances full of gorgeous men, magic, twists, and cliffhangers that she hopes her readers enjoy reading as much as she enjoys writing them.

Alice currently lives in Asia with her cat dreaming up, writing down, and living in her next book alongside her characters ...

Follow Alice Wilde on Facebook/ Amazon to stay up to date with new releases.

Connect with Alice
   Email: **alicewildeauthor@gmail.com**
   Tiktok: **@aliceWildeauthor**

 facebook.com/AliceWildeAuthor
 instagram.com/alice_wilde_author

Printed in Great Britain
by Amazon